GLOSSARY
FOR THE
END OF DAYS

GLOSSARY
FOR THE
END OF DAYS

STORIES

IAN STANSEL

ACRE

CINCINNATI 2020

Acre Books is made possible by the support of the Robert and Adele Schiff Foundation and the Department of English at the University of Cincinnati.

Designed by Barbara Neely Bourgoyne

ISBN-13 (pbk) 978-1-946724-34-2
ISBN-13 (ebook) 978-1-946724-35-9

The press is based at the University of Cincinnati, Department of English and Comparative Literature, McMicken Hall, Room 248, PO Box 210069, Cincinnati, OH, 45221–0069. www.acre-books.com

Acre Books books may be purchased at a discount for educational use. For information please email business@acre-books.com.

for Travis

CONTENTS

. . . .

ONE

JOHN IS ALIVE

. . . .

My cousin and I were just fifteen, standing in the cold outside the big Tower Records on Mercer, waiting to buy the new Beatles album. Everyone was there. Parent types, old hippies, the punks and surfers and skate kids. Black folks, white folks, Asian and Hispanic folks. The record was set to come out at midnight, and the damp Seattle air was electric, everyone buzzing to hear what the four boys from Liverpool had made for the world after all this time. Other people had thought to bring blankets and ponchos and the like, but of course Natasha and I hadn't, so we stood leaning into one another as the temperature dropped with the evening sun. She was wearing her jean jacket buttoned up all the way, and I had my Members Only zipped and snapped around my pencil neck. She put an arm around my shoulders, but still we were shivering by nine o'clock.

Natasha and I were both born in the summer of 1970, only a month apart, not long after Paul made it official that the band was breaking up. Maybe that was one of the reasons Natasha and I were so excited about the new record. We had never lived in a world where the Beatles existed. We'd just missed them. Still, we'd spent most of our free time sprawled on the rug in her parents' place in Forest Hill, listening to *Help!* and *Abbey Road* and *Revolver*—Natasha's favorite. We followed their solo careers, she being more sympathetic to George's morose spirituality, and I far more forgiving of Paul's sugary crooning. We both rooted for

Ringo and found John to be the most baffling of the group. She and I swooned and swayed to "Mind Games" and "#9 Dream" and thought "Gimme Some Truth" was the world's first punk song. A couple years before, in eighth grade, Natasha played "Imagine" for her end-of-year piano recital. And we both cried endlessly in the hours after the shooting when it looked like John wouldn't make it. Natasha's estimation of Paul went up when it came out that he was there along with Yoko at John's bedside for those hours and days before his eyes reopened. The moment the two of them, along with John's doctor, walked to a bouquet of microphones outside Roosevelt Hospital and announced that John would be ok, it was as if the world had somehow righted itself again.

Around ten o'clock, Natasha rubbed her arms and said, "I need to warm up. Why's it always so fucking freezing in this stupid city?" We told ourselves we hated Seattle because of the damp and cold, but really we hated it because it was home—the same reason I would love and long for it years later.

Natasha ducked under a yellow sawhorse, one of a couple dozen that kept the line contained against the wall of the shop. A dude a few spots behind us called out, "You get out of the line, you gotta go to the back." He was maybe thirty, with long hair and a beard and weathered skin and a general Charles Manson kind of vibe.

"Are you serious?" Natasha said. "I'm just going to pee."

"Can I watch?" the dude said. A couple other guys made shows of muffling their chuckles with fists.

Natasha looked at me for a second, but I was useless, a skinny, acne-ridden not-man. "You'd like that, you gross old perv," she said to the dude. She turned and strode into the store, leaving me to be glanced at by the others. Most of the time I could pretend I wasn't still a kid, like when we bummed around Broadway or took the bus out to Pike Place. But there, up against the wall of the record store, I felt tiny. A pathetic little tadpole.

. . . .

In addition to being born so close together, Natasha and I were also both only-children, so early on we became almost like siblings and looked out for one another. My parents talked to each other only when necessary, Dad retreating to his office on the second floor to read books on the Revolutionary War, and Mom sitting at the small table in the kitchen for hours smoking Merits and tapping a fingernail against the Formica; I couldn't imagine what she was thinking of. Natasha's folks— my Aunt Shelly and Uncle Mike—seemed to like each other a bit better than mine. Spirituality was their bag, and they went on countless retreats in Snoqualmie and sometimes even down to Sedona to work on their chakras and practice being present. At home, they lit candles and meditated, neglecting their daughter in the name of allowing her to cultivate independence. For Natasha and me, the records we loved were bursts of beautiful noise in an otherwise muted world.

Then right about when we turned thirteen Natasha seemed to change. It was as if a darkness took over her. She talked less and would stare at a page of whatever book she had with her for minutes on end, never flipping to the next.

"You're not even reading that," I would say, and she would snap out of it.

"Oh, sorry."

"Sorry for what?" I'd say, not a little shittily.

"I don't know," she'd say, her voice barely audible. Then she would go back to her page.

The sadness she began carrying was one I feared and for some reason resented. Maybe because I'd learned from my parents that sadness and disappointment were inevitable parts of being an adult, and Natasha taking up those traits at our young age only reminded me of what was coming. Or maybe I was just lazy and empathically deficient. Either way, I stopped hanging out with her so much and retreated to my fellow boys so I could talk endlessly about movies and tv shows and, of course, the Beatles. But when I told my mom I wanted to camp out for the new album, she suggested I bring my cousin.

"Mom," I whined. "We don't hang out anymore."

She told me to ask Natasha or I couldn't go, so I kicked the kitchen wall and said, "Fine."

• • • •

Natasha was in the store a good twenty minutes. I guessed she was spinning something in one of the listening booths, so I smoked a couple cigarettes, trying to age myself. Just as I had been doing for weeks, the people around me speculated on what the album would be like. Would there be synths, like on the Wings records? Would John break out some dirty blues? Would Yoko be on it? Linda? What would George contribute?

Someone in the group in front of me said, "I heard Ringo's got three vocal tracks, man."

"No way," I said. The idea was so ludicrous I spoke before my social anxiety could stop me.

All of them, three guys and two girls, probably seventeen, maybe eighteen, looked back at me. "What I heard, kid," the one who'd made the claim said.

"He's only got one song on the *White Album*, and that's like thirty songs long or whatever. It's gonna be one Ringo, two George and the rest John and Paul," I said. "Like it should be."

"Guess we'll see," a girl said. "In T-minus ninety minutes." She was lean and freckled and pretty in a long-faced kind of way. She and Natasha shared a style—both were throwback summer girls with tattered blue jeans and rock t-shirts, long hair free of sprays and mousses. No jelly bracelets or Swatches for them. No Simon Le Bon fedoras or Material Girl scrunchies. I turned away and lit another cigarette, even though my lungs ached from the others. When Natasha finally came back out, she swung her legs over the sawhorse, said "Hey," and—though I knew she was trying not to—looked back at the dude with the Manson vibe who'd been giving her shit before.

"Everything come out ok?" the old perv said. Natasha gave him the finger, then looked at me, mashed up her face and rolled her eyes.

Around eleven someone lit a joint and then all of a sudden the reefer floodgates opened and joints were getting passed up and down the line like kind words. The girl in the group in front of us handed me one and said, "You're probably right about Ringo. But he had two on the *White Album*. You're forgetting 'Goodnight.'"

"Well, John wrote it," I said.

"Still, though," she said. "What's your name?"

"Cal," I told her.

"I'm Denise."

Natasha made a point of introducing herself as my cousin. When Denise turned back to her friends, Natasha elbowed me in the ribs and waggled her eyebrows. I shook my head and averted my eyes, though I liked Natasha teasing me. It felt like back when we were kids.

At a quarter to twelve the energy in line started to rise. We were all stoned, but the wide grins cutting across our faces now seemed to be less the result of the THC permeating our bodies and more about the record we'd all soon hold in our hands.

A man came out of Tower and boomed, "All right, folks, we're going to do a countdown, New Year's Eve–style, and when we get to zero the record is for sale. We've got it behind the counter, so no one go roaming around the store being all, 'I just want to grab the new Prince.'

Come in in an orderly fashion, go straight to the counter, and tell the cashier how many. It's one or two. No more. You say 'one' or you say 'two.' And then you pay. And then you leave. Clear?"

We said "clear," and the guy grinned and nodded and turned back into the store. Sure enough, not long after, we found ourselves counting down from ten with unembarrassed enthusiasm. At "Four!" Natasha knocked her hip into mine and did a little hop. After "One!" we all cheered and the manager opened the door and started ushering people to the counter. Natasha and I shuffled forward, her saying things like "so rad" partly to me, partly, I imagine, to whatever gods ruled over music and dope and nights like these.

We finally entered the warmth of the store and got to the counter. "Two," Natasha said to the chick manning the register. The girl tapped at the keys and we gave her our money and she bagged our LPs. Outside, we could hardly hold in our giddiness. Natasha squeezed my shoulder, digging her thin fingers in. In the parking lot we pulled our records from the bag and examined the front and back covers. On the front was a simple shot of them all peering into the camera. Natasha and I agreed that it was a lot like *Rubber Soul*, though brighter, more summery. Here they looked happy.

I was just about to examine the song titles and credits on the back when I heard the girl named Denise say, "Two from Ringo." I looked to where she stood with her friends. She was smiling at me. "We're going over to my friend's place to listen to it; you guys want to come?"

It was past midnight, late even for us, who never had too much in the way of supervision. But Natasha said to me, "I'm not going home," so I turned to Denise and said, "Sure."

"Cool," Denise said.

· · · ·

A whole pack of us made our way up Fifth Ave and swung a left down Aloha. Natasha hooked my arm and leaned close to me. "You're totally getting laid tonight," she said.

I rolled my eyes, then watched her. I asked, "Have you?" though most of me didn't want to know the answer.

"What? Oh my god," she said with a snort. But her levity didn't last. Her mouth fell and her eyes went to stone and she said to me, "You can't ask someone that." She let go of my arm but stayed close. "You have no idea what it's like being a girl," she said, her tone now bordering on despair.

"What is it like?"

She exhaled a long breath and eyed the buildings looming above us. "It's awful," she said. "It's so fucking awful."

We all stopped at an apartment building maybe seven stories high. One of the guys in Denise's crew, this guy Marco, went in, and we watched through the glass door as he bounded up the staircase. Denise bummed a cigarette from me. I thought about lighting it for her, but worried that would come off as creepy or cheesy. After a second, she lit it herself.

"So you two are cousins," she said. "That's cool. Like, cousins who hang out together."

"That's us," Natasha said. "Thick as thieves, me and this slick motherfucker."

Denise laughed. "I got some cousins, but they're in Florida," she said. "And they're like older or whatever. I have a sister, too, but she's a full-on bitch. Where do you guys go to school?"

We told her and she said she was a senior and in the fall she'd be heading to U-Dub, the same place I would end up two years later. I nodded and hoped she wouldn't ask me what year I was in school, the word "sophomore" suddenly seeming so puny and embarrassing.

After five minutes, Marco came back down the stairs and out the door, shaking his head slowly the whole way. "No go," he said. "Parents are home." We all deflated a bit. Some of his friends started giving him shit. "I mean," he said, "we could go up to the roof. No music, but we could smoke a cheech. And I could probably pilfer a few beers from the fridge."

If Natasha and I left then, we probably wouldn't get to our houses until almost one. Too late to listen to the album anyway. Plus, there was Denise. I liked the dream world I was developing in my head where she and I ended up making out, and I didn't want that shattered quite yet. So we followed the others up seven flights of stairs, Marco shushing us every few steps, and then up a ten-rung ladder attached to the wall, and through a hatch to the roof.

All around us the city was dark. I could just barely make out, between two buildings, a wedge of moonlit Mount Rainier. Denise came to me. "Is this where you thought you'd end up tonight?" she said. "On some stranger's roof?"

"Of course," I said.

"You can see the future then, I guess."

I nodded. She said, "Well, in that case, I might have some questions later."

Marco, who'd gone back down, now emerged once again, his head popping up from the hatch opening. He swung a six-pack onto the gravel roof and then hoisted the rest of his body through. I watched as two more people followed, dismayed as it registered that the second of these men was the old perv from the line at Tower.

"Fucking great," Natasha muttered.

"He's mostly harmless," Denise said, apparently intuiting the gist of what had happened earlier.

"Maybe we should just go," I said to Natasha.

"No way," she said. "We're not letting that gross old fuck dictate what we do."

Denise said, "Damn right, girl."

On the upside, the old perv and his probably-just-as-pervy friend—who dressed like Damone from *Fast Times*—brought more beer. Denise went and pulled a few, brought them back. We drank and looked out over the city. We talked about the Beatles, citing our favorite songs, debating who'd had the best solo career. Natasha and Denise quickly agreed on John, though both wished George had spread *All Things Must Pass* out over at least a couple records. He'd shot his wad too quick was the consensus.

"Paul is Cal's man," Natasha said. "Always has been. I remember you singing 'Good Day Sunshine' and 'Silly Love Songs' for*ever*."

"Aww," Denise said sweetly. "Those are the worst songs."

"They're not," I said, strategizing that I might as well stick to my guns. "Everyone will see. History will prove me right."

"Telling the future again?" Denise said.

"You'll see," I told her.

The weed and beer were really hitting me now, and I felt like a balloon filled with perfectly warm water. Maybe Natasha and Denise were feeling that way too because we all three went silent for a long time. I thought vaguely about how it was possible to be so happy and so sad at the same time. Then Natasha said, "Can you imagine if that crazy piece of shit had really killed John?"

I shook my head slowly and imagined Denise was doing the same, though I couldn't seem to take my eyes from the most beautiful splatter of paint on the lip of the roof. So zoned out was I that I hadn't noticed the old perv sidling up to us.

"Don't think he didn't," he said, startling each of us from our stoned fugue. "That man shot and killed John Lennon, same way Paul died in that car wreck in '66."

"And I guess the people on the new record are imposters," Denise said.

"No," the old perv said. "They're them. In this version of reality, anyway. In some other version, there is no record. No Beatles. And in some other version, there never was a Beatles, because none of them were ever even born."

"Oh good," Natasha said. "Stoner talk."

"You can believe what you want," he said. "Think that this is the only reality. Go ahead. But this shit's been proven with math, man. Every split-second splinters off into infinite versions of the world. You know how they say the universe is expanding? It's the same with reality. On some other plane, those bullets hit Johnny Boy square in the heart, and he was dead instantly. In that version, none of us are here, 'cause there's no record. Hell, in some other version, this building isn't even here. This city. Even us. We don't exist."

"That version is sounding pretty good right now," Natasha said. Denise laughed, but the old perv didn't miss a beat.

"And in another version," he continued, "Chapman didn't even fire the gun. He chickened out. And in that one, there was no reason for Paul to come help John, and so they never got back together. We just happen to be living in this particular version. So we get the record. You see what I'm saying?"

He pulled a joint from his shirt pocket and lit it, passed it to Denise, who took a puff. She offered it to Natasha and me, but my cousin waved it off, so I did too.

"They proved this?" Denise asked.

"Damn right," he said.

The old perv took another drag and then turned to walk away. As he did, he said, "There's a version of reality where I'm the biggest fucking rock star in the world." He did an air guitar solo and kept walking.

Denise wandered over to her friends, and Natasha and I watched the clouds overhead, which seemed almost within reach, lit up from below by the city. "Thanks for asking me to come tonight," Natasha said. "I know you didn't want me here."

"Yes, I did," I lied. "What are you talking about?"

She let out a breath, said, "It's fine." She moved a Chuck Taylor in an arc across the pebbles on the roof. "This has been such a fun night," she said after a long silence.

"Yeah," I agreed.

She lit another cigarette. "Can I tell you something?" she said. "I'm getting out of here."

"You want to go home?"

She shook her head. "Out of this city. I've been saving up."

"What are you talking about? Running away?"

"*Quietly turning the backdoor key,*" she sang. "*Stepping outside, she is free.*"

"Shut up," I said. "Where?"

"San Francisco," she said. "Maybe New York."

"New York?" I said, terrified, marveling at the thought.

"I don't know. Anywhere but here." She finally looked at me. "You want to come with me? Think about it. It's not like our parents give a shit about us."

"Mine do," I said weakly.

"Believe what you want," she said.

Some of the guys in Denise's gang started attempting handstands, alternately helping each other stay vertical and pushing each other down, everyone laughing as their friends hit the deck.

"Seriously," I said to Natasha. "Are you just fucking with me?"

"I don't know," she said teasingly. "Are you gonna come with me?"

"No," I said. "We're kids."

She smiled with the side of her mouth. "Well, then it's a good thing I'm just fucking with you, kid."

I told myself I believed her because it was easier that way, but it pissed me off, the way she had brought her melancholy to what had up until that moment been a good night. "What's *wrong* with you?" I said.

Her face fell into an expression of terrible shock and hurt. "Nothing," she said. "There's nothing wrong with me, Cal." She walked to the opposite end of the roof to where Marco stood.

A few minutes later Denise and I ended up sitting against some kind of air conditioning or heating unit, the gravel digging into my bony ass every time I shifted, while Natasha talked with Marco and the old perv. "You know," Denise said to me, "there's another realm of reality where you understand how bad 'Silly Love Songs' is."

She told me about her parents and how they thought she was at a friend's house, staying overnight. She said she couldn't wait until next year when she'd be out on her own. She said more, but I didn't hear most of it. I watched Natasha, at the other end of the roof, run a hand through her hair, her foot up on the edge. Denise must have caught on to my distraction, because she said, "Your cousin is really pretty."

People talked a lot about how beautiful Natasha was. I usually didn't notice or think about it; she was just my cousin, almost my sister. There on the roof, though, half drunk and fully stoned, my everyday eyes removed and replaced with a set far more clear and strange, she looked so beautiful and so damn lonely it scared me.

Denise got my attention back, told me I could kiss her if I wanted to. "Maybe you'll be the last high school boy I ever kiss," she said. She would be the first high school girl I'd kiss. The first and last time I'd connected my lips with a girl's was in eighth grade, a time that felt so long ago it might as well have been one of the old perv's other dimensions. We touched lips and the metallic zing of the beer we'd been drinking floated on Denise's breath.

Because of the kiss, my eyes were closed when Natasha disappeared over the edge of the building. I only heard voices issue loud, urgent nonsense. Shouts. A scream. When Denise and I parted our mouths, my cousin was gone. For an interminable second I thought she was hiding, playing some game we'd long ago given up. Then people crept toward where Marco and the old perv stood, where Natasha had been just a moment before, and peered over the side. I stood and joined them. "Oh my god," Denise said, the situation just becoming clear.

Marco panted, "I think it was the rocks. Her foot must have slipped."

The old perv looked like he was going to fall over himself. "I reached out, man," he said to me, his eyes desperate. "I almost had her."

I stayed away from the edge, unable to bring myself to look down, to see the proof of what had just happened. My mind powerless to find a way to reverse time.

• • • •

An hour later we watched the old perv getting put into the back of a cop car, but he was only getting hauled in for corrupting us kids. No one said my cousin had been pushed. Everyone's version was the same. She just . . . fell. Didn't even make a sound. I told the police and my parents and Natasha's parents everything they wanted to know. The line at Tower, the pot, the roof, the beer. I told them what Natasha had said about running away. "But she was joking," I insisted. "She was messing with me." At some point I'd picked up Natasha's Beatles record from where she'd left it on the roof, and down on the street I held both of our copies to my chest as Natasha's body was put into the blinding white of an ambulance.

It wasn't until a month later that Aunt Shelly read Natasha's diary, and it came out what Uncle Mike had been doing to Natasha. *Inappropriate* was the word my parents used when I threw a glass against the wall and demanded they tell me what everyone was whispering about. He'd been *inappropriate* with her. My parents wouldn't elaborate,

15

wouldn't move beyond that word, would only repeat it over and over, and it was only after the hundredth time that I let myself understand what it meant. People started to use the word *jump*—an idea I still try not to believe. But I think back to that night, what Natasha said it was like being a girl. *Awful*, she'd said. *It's so fucking awful.*

No one seemed to know what to do, not my aunt, not my parents, not the police—not even with the diary or even after Uncle Mike stopped denying what had happened and simply went silent. It soon became clear that the cops wouldn't do a thing—Natasha had never said anything to anyone, and she wasn't around to make the allegation herself—so Aunt Shelly wept for days on end in our living room, sleeping on our couch, smoking cigarettes, and eating Saltine crackers slathered with deviled ham spread. She seemed to forget all about meditation routines and chakras. I imagine she was present, though—probably more present than she'd ever been in her life. Before long, Uncle Mike simply disappeared from our lives, moving—I heard later—to Denver, and Aunt Shelly sold their house and moved to Portland and became an alcoholic until she found God and started sending me little cards with pictures of Jesus on them. She and my mom drifted apart and quit talking except on Thanksgiving. After a few years, even that ended, and my aunt vanished, too.

I never did open the records Natasha and I bought that night.

• • • •

All of this happened, but I like to think that there are other versions of reality. There are versions where Natasha didn't die. Like the one where the old perv's hand got hold of the collar of her jean jacket and he pulled her back and everyone up on the roof said "Oh, man!" and "Holy shit!" and took extra care when they descended the rungs of the ladder to go home, recognizing how close one of us came to tragedy.

Or the one where we never even went up to that roof or the one where my Uncle Mike didn't molest his daughter in the first place. There is a version where I hadn't let the petty waters of adolescence erode the bonds between us, where Natasha asked me to run away with her to San Francisco or New York and I said, "Yes. Anywhere. Let's go."

And there is a reality I hold in my mind even now, decades later, where Natasha does fall, does die, but here John Lennon is also dead because in this one Chapman's bullets did their job, killed him. Here Natasha and John Lennon meet—after all, if there are other dimensions, who's to say there isn't an afterlife too? Natasha tells John Lennon about all the times she and her cousin swayed to "Mind Games" and "#9 Dream" and how the two of them had decided that "Gimme Some Truth" was the first punk song. She tells him about how close she and her cousin had been, how they loved each other. And she tells him about the time she played his song for her eighth grade piano recital and how everyone in the audience, the adults and kids alike, wept for all the things they could imagine but couldn't make real.

NORTH OUT OF HOUSTON

. . . .

Each of the three members of the Vallely family slouched against their respective car door. They had been in this spot for an hour. And in the hour before this one, they'd moved a half mile, if that. Behind them the Houston skyline rose like a triumph against bad odds and better judgment, the city so low and flat that the roads flooded in even the most routine late-summer storms, a city so close to the coast that the worse storms, the nonroutine, had become routine. A five-hundred-year storm was bearing down on the coast just a hundred miles south of the Vallely family's Subaru—the second such storm in the past decade.

Kip Vallely sat in the driver's seat, Joanna Vallely in the passenger, and Denny Vallely, their fourteen-year-old son, sat in the back, having unclipped his seatbelt a good forty-five minutes before. Kip had thought to tell him to put it back on, then realized how ridiculous that would sound. They weren't going anywhere.

"It's like that song," Kip now said. "The video with the traffic."

Joanna knew what he meant. The old REM video where people in a traffic jam start to sing and bond over their shared woes.

"Or that movie," she said.

"Which movie?"

"The musical," she said. "They're stuck on the highway, and everyone gets out and dances and sings."

Kip squinted his eyes at the Ford in front of them. He had no idea what she was talking about. "I have no idea what you're talking about," he told her.

Joanna sighed. "We watched it," she said.

"What was it called?"

"I'm blanking on it," Joanna said.

"*La La Land*," Denny said, his voice soaked in exasperation.

"*La La Land*?" Kip said. "I've never seen *La La Land*."

"Oh my god!" Denny said, tossing his head back.

"We watched it together," Joanna said. "The three of us. A month ago. You made popcorn."

Kip shook his head slowly. "Nope," he said.

Behind him, Denny let out a burst of laughter. Kip felt good to be able to make him laugh, even if he had to sacrifice himself by playing the fool. The next exit was another three miles up, and even the shoulder had become clogged with cars. A laugh felt like a tiny escape.

Joanna looked, for perhaps the twentieth time, at the woman in the car next to her. It was some kind of Volkswagen, she thought. The woman—young, with short, dark hair lightened at the tips—scrolled her thumb across her phone screen. In the backseat was a baby, sleeping. Joanna flipped down the visor and opened the mirror to look at her son in the backseat. "How are you doing, sweetheart?" she said, turning in her seat.

Denny looked at her, then tapped at his phone and pulled his headphones off his ears.

"What?"

"What are you listening to?"

"Nothing."

"Nothing?"

"A podcast," he said.

"What's it about?"

"Just stupid celebrity stuff," he said. "It's funny. There's a guy and he goes around places like New York and asks people on the street questions about celebrities." He laughed to himself, remembering one particular bit that had tickled him. "Like, asking old people about Nicki Minaj or whatever."

"You should be reading books," Kip said. "The great books! Thoreau and Dickens and Melville."

It was Kip's way of joking, giving Denny a hard time about the frivolity of the younger generation. Joanna knew it was all in jest, but she couldn't help but feel the urge to come to her son's defense. "He does read," she said. "Anyway, what was the last book you finished?"

"I read the Keith Richards one."

"The great books!" Joanna mocked. She looked back at Denny and grinned, but he didn't reciprocate. Instead his eyes went back to his phone, and the headphones went back over his ears.

Joanna felt certain that Denny existed somewhere on the queer spectrum. He'd always been shy and slightly effeminate, even as a younger kid, eschewing sports and other male-dominated endeavors in favor of books and even for a short time cross-stitching. And not long ago she'd found a couple of her blouses, ones she'd set aside for Goodwill, in his drawer, as well as a smashed lipstick she'd tossed in the bathroom trash. Joanna understood that her child was finding himself—herself? themself?—and that this would take time. But was she just using sensitivity and respect as an excuse to avoid dealing with this aspect of her child's life? A hundred times she'd meant to talk to him about his burgeoning identity, but each time she felt a speech welling up in her— Judith Butler and gender as performance and the reductive natures of categories—it wasn't what he needed, she told herself. Or maybe it was. Maybe he needed that speech, or maybe he just needed time. Or maybe he needed a therapist, or maybe she should have them all start going to some Unitarian church with a sweet old lesbian minister. Or maybe she should simply take the parental controls off the internet and let him go hog wild with all the various permutations of gender and sexuality possible, see where his eyes and heart lingered. The fact was that for all her philosophy and theory, all her books, even her own goddamn experiences, she still didn't have a clue what he needed, and not knowing made her anxious, and so she'd done nothing, which made her feel like a failure as a parent.

Up the road a bit, a truck driver and another man, who'd gotten out of a minivan, were straddling the dashed line talking. Kip adjusted the rearview to see another group who'd left their cars. "People are getting out."

"I'm surprised it took this long," Joanna said, following the trend and getting out herself, shutting the door behind her.

Kip felt uncertain, though he didn't know why. The idea of standing on a highway, even one as stuck as this, felt strange and dangerous. He watched his wife reach high above her and then bend into half-moon pose. He liked watching her do her yoga in the mornings, though he hoped not in a totally creepy way. She'd taken up the habit soon after moving back in and getting off the booze, and in the six months since then she'd dropped a good ten pounds, maybe fifteen. Not that her weight was ever a problem for him—in fact, he'd always enjoyed the little bit of softness she carried. It was more that the weight reflected something more, a shedding of the anxiety and anger that had built up between them over the course of seventeen years of marriage. He hoped so, anyway.

Kip turned to Denny, caught his eye, and the boy removed one of his headphones. "I know this is frustrating," Kip said. "I'm sure it'll start moving soon."

"No it won't," Denny said. "We're going to be here forever. We're gonna have to, like, eat that baby over there." He nodded to the VW in the next lane.

"For chrissake," Kip said. "Don't talk about eating babies."

"I was just kidding," Denny said, tossing his headphones on the seat next to his phone and opening the door.

"Be careful out there, please," Kip said as his son stepped out. He imagined some motorcyclist pushed beyond the breaking point speeding up between the cars and blasting Denny off like a foul ball.

Outside, Joanna had one foot out in front of her in a lunging pose and a hand reaching toward the sky. Denny saw people in their cars watching.

"What's that?" Denny said.

"Reverse warrior," Joanna said through the strain of her stretch. Denny eyed the compacted bump of his mother's butt above her elongated leg.

"Why do you do it?" Denny said.

His mother straightened. "Yoga? It keeps me centered. Keeps my mind focused."

"I thought that's what the meetings were for."

Joanna watched her son with new intensity, then relaxed. She hated talking about her drinking with Denny, but she also knew that talking about it was part of the deal. The AA deal and the deal she'd made with Kip when he took her back. "The meetings deal with a specific issue," she said.

"Your alcoholism," Denny offered.

Joanna took a shallow breath, said in a soft voice, "Yes. And yoga helps more holistically."

More people were getting out of their cars, shaking the stiffness from their limbs.

"How come people always do it in public?" Denny said.

"They don't."

"Mostly, though. Going to a park or taking classes. I mean, people take classes for years, right? But, like, how long does it take to master the fucking downward dog?"

"Hey," Joanna said. "Watch the language."

"It's just to be seen. Like, 'Look what I can do. Look at me standing on one foot. Look at my butt.' I mean, you know all these dudes in cars are watching you."

"I don't care if anyone is watching me," Joanna said.

"Whatever."

"What's the problem, hon?"

"Nothing." Denny held her gaze.

She set a hand on her hip, and her eyes went all sympathetic in that condescending way they did. "You know you can talk to me, right?" she said. "About anything."

Denny shrugged. He knew what she wanted, for him to ask her questions—like he was one of those clients of hers who thought they were sad only because they were too smart to be happy. She wanted him to come to her for guidance, to ask questions. God, the looks he got from her. Help me, she wanted him to say.

Or maybe that wasn't fair. Maybe she did just want to listen, to be a mom. And of course he did need help—who didn't?—but not the kind she thought he needed. Parents always thought whatever they experienced explained the whole world.

"I'm taking a walk," he said.

"Hey," Joanna said, but her son was already striding away, heading back toward the skyline. Joanna thought for a moment about going after him, but figured he'd go a few hundred yards, make whatever point he needed to make, and then come back on his own.

Joanna leaned her back against the Subaru. She had the sudden urge for a cigarette. She hadn't had one in fifteen years, but if there was a time to break the good streak, it was now, wasn't it? Standing on a highway, stuck in place while trying to outrun the ninety-mile-an-hour winds of a tropical storm?

Joanna was a philosophical therapist, something she'd never heard of until she did, until her work at a relatively well-established counseling office in the Heights neighborhood started to seem empty and unproductive. She'd been at it for just over a decade and figured that that anniversary, the false significance of the ten-year mark, had something to do with her crisis of vocational faith. It was then that she started to revisit the worn, dog-eared paperback copies of Hume and Kant, of Butler and Burke, the books that had so excited her synapses as an undergrad, before she redirected herself—with the encouragement of her parents, neither of whom had attended college and who were baffled by her choice of major at Rice—to something more practical. In grad school at Baylor she took up counseling and, three years later, began the good work of helping people face their anxieties, obsessions, fears, and destructive choices—or at least make peace with the ever-presence of those little bugaboos.

Her disenchantment with the traditional approach coincided with her first glimmer of understanding of her own addictions, and she was forced to wonder if she really believed all of that talking about her clients' inner lives was doing any good. She watched them come and go, returning or disappearing completely. She herself had seen three different therapists over the years and, more often than not, chased each session with increasing amounts of vodka. She wondered if there might be another way.

Or perhaps she just wanted to feel special. Sure, you could find a hundred perfectly competent counselors without leaving the 610 loop, all eager to become codependent with you, but how many could do what she did? Who could relate your trials to Schopenhauer and Hegel? Plus, with a philosophical foundation to the therapy, she made no claims about the likelihood of making her clients feel better. In fact, their sadnesses often only became deeper. And yet they came back, all of them, week after week, year after year.

Joanna looked through the Subaru's window to see Kip spinning the wheel on his iPod Classic, looking, she knew, for that REM song. She popped up from the side of the car and began walking up the highway, the opposite way as her son.

• • • •

Denny moved between the cars, some of the people behind the windshields eyeing him as he passed, but most pointed their gazes crotchward, staring at their phones. Denny realized the mistake he'd made in taking this walk. There was something he wanted to not think about, and all of the previous afternoon and evening and night, as well as that morning, he'd been successful only when distracting himself. Now, with his own phone back in the car, there was nothing to keep his mind from the thought.

The day before, the Vallelys were making final preparations to flee the city. NPR played constantly in the background, reporting on the storm's progress. The car was all but completely packed with clothes and irreplaceables (heirloom jewelry, family photos, some of Kip's rarer records). Denny was in the kitchen making peanut butter and jelly sandwiches and setting them atop the cans of bubbly water in a cooler. His parents were upstairs. Denny could hear them talking in that calm way they had taken up since Joanna moved back six months before. Every word measured, considered, and spoken in a put-on serene way that made Denny think of his most pretentious classmates, the way they would speak softly in class when commenting on "The Yellow Wallpaper" in order to make them seem oh so thoughtful. English teachers ate that shit up. Meanwhile Denny was stuck leaning forward into the hard edge of the desk and cupping his ears just to make out what they were saying. It drove him crazy. And now his parents were doing it. Denny figured it was better than the fighting and extended silences of before. But still. There was no way to be comfortable with those voices, like people who would come into a room but never sit down.

As he set the last sandwich in the cooler, a phone buzzed. His mother's phone, sitting on the counter. Denny glanced at the screen, alighted with a text message. No name, just a number and the words *Sure you have to leave town?* The screen went dark, useless except to reflect Denny's peering face. But then it lit up again. *I got that itch baby.*

Denny stared at himself in the screen after it went black. He pressed the button on the side of her phone and saw the messages again. He read them over and over, trying to force them to mean something other than what was plainly and devastatingly clear. In the cooler at his feet, a cluster of ice cubes broke apart, and everything on top collapsed and fell askew.

· · · ·

Four months before the storm, Joanna found herself getting increasingly creeped out by a couple of the lurkers at her usual AA meeting and decided to try one in Montrose. She sat at the back, as she normally did, and studied her fingernails, as she normally did, waiting for the moment when the meeting leader would ask for the hands of any newcomers to the group. As the room filled up, she listened to the people around her greet one another with handshakes and slaps on the back. "Staying sober today?" they'd ask one another, and then answer, "One hour at a time, one day at a time," and then, "That's it, that's all you can do." It was the same at all of the meetings she'd been to, and that was part of the comfort. The interchangeability of the people reminded her that no one was particularly different or special, that she herself was not different or special. She liked that. Rather than striking a blow to her ego, this reminder bolstered her understanding that she was failing no more than anyone else. Just failing in her own way.

Kirsten was there that first evening, in the multipurpose room of an Episcopal church. "Hey," she said to Joanna after the meeting. People were helping to fold up the chairs, forming a line to stack them.

"Hey."

"I'm the official greeter of any new people who look like they might be cool," Kirsten said.

"And I made the cut?" Joanna said with feigned honor.

They got coffee that night and then again the next week and then lunch on a Tuesday at a French bistro where they ate croque monsieurs and sipped after-meal espresso. Kirsten had her elbows on the small table when she said, "I took the whole afternoon off."

Since that day, they'd been meeting at Kirsten's apartment in the Museum District twice a week. Aside from a confusing flirtation with a girl during graduate school—a flirtation that never went anywhere—this was the first time she'd ever been in a relationship with a woman. It was terrifying and thrilling at first, then after three or four times together, the fear faded while the thrill remained. They drank tea and made love and watched YouTube clips in bed. Joanna was teaching Kirsten yoga and trying to get her to quit smoking. Kirsten talked about running for city council. After a month Joanna knew she was falling in love with Kirsten, falling in a way she never had with Kip, with anyone. She thought about her constantly, counting the moments until their next meeting, imagining her face, her voice, her body. The feel of her hands on Joanna's skin, the light drag of her nails down her neck, across her shoulders. Her stomach dropped and tumbled at the thought of her. Yes, this was love, rapturous and destructive and all-consuming. And she was not unaware of the irony, that if she hadn't come back to Kip and agreed to his demand that she attend AA, she never would have met the woman.

. . . .

Kip was listening to his music with eyes closed when a horn bleated behind him. The Ford in front of them had moved forward, leaving a gap of five or six car lengths.

"Shit," Kip said. He scanned the outside of the car. No Joanna, no Denny. Of course. "Goddamn it," he said. The car behind—a Dodge Charger—honked again, and Kip put the car in drive, rolled forward a few yards, then stopped. Where was he going? He couldn't leave his wife and son there on the highway. Why hadn't he watched which way they went, and why the hell had they gone anywhere anyway? He shifted back into park and got out. The guy in the Charger behind put his palms up, international sign language for *The fuck, man?*

"I know, I know," Kip muttered, jogging to the passenger side, peering up and down the aisle between lanes.

"Hey, guy," the other man said, his head halfway out the window.

"My kid wandered off," Kip said.

The man dropped his head in exasperation. The woman in his passenger seat shook her head and lit a cigarette.

"Denny!" Kip called though cupped hands.

The VW with the woman and the baby cut over into the space in front of the Subaru. "Come on!" the man behind called. Kip didn't know what to do, didn't want to go anywhere, but collapsed under the pressure of the man's voice and glare. He got back in the car and started forward at a crawl, opening all the windows and calling out for his wife and child.

Movement didn't last long, though. Not a hundred yards up they were back at a stop. After a moment, to confirm the new stasis, Kip got back out into the heat and humidity. He eyed the man behind, said, "Happy?" and stepped back toward the space between lanes.

"What?" the man said, getting out. He was bigger than Kip and moved with the authority of a person who lived a physical life, one wildly different from Kip's world of software development. The man strode toward Kip. "What'd you say?"

Kip decided to stay firm. Yes, despite his suddenly hammering heart he'd stay firm and soften only once he'd gained the man's respect. Maybe Kip would offer him a LaCroix. "I said 'Are you happy?' We moved up twenty feet."

The man shoved Kip backward with such sudden force that his feet were barely able to keep him from toppling. Kip's body went hot with fear as he decided that the person once again inching toward him was maybe not a LaCroix man.

Kip's pummeling—which would have been his first since seventh grade—was halted only by the voice of the woman in the Charger. "Tommy," she said. "What the fuck are you doing?"

The man—Tommy—put a finger up toward Kip's nose. "Watch it, you little faggot." Everyone around them was staring, looking at Kip just standing there, petrified in place. After a moment, he saw Denny coming toward him between cars. Behind his son, dark clouds had begun to enshroud the city.

• • • •

"Jesus," Joanna said, now back in the car and twisted sideways in her seat to face Kip. Kip had just recounted the incident with the man in the Charger.

"Yeah," Kip said. "Guy was nuts."

Denny turned to the back window. Joanna said, "Don't."

"Why not?" Denny said. "We shouldn't let bigots be comfortable."

"I know," Joanna said. "You're right. But we also don't want to court danger."

"Court danger?" Denny said. He rolled his eyes.

"Invite it," Joanna said.

"I know what it means."

"Your mother's right," Kip said. "Just leave it alone."

"That's how these people get away with it," Denny said.

"Just, please," Joanna said. She looked out her window. The VW with the sleeping baby was in front of them now, and beside them was a Prius with two women in it. Their profiles—pointy noses over slightly weak chins—were identical, and Joanna decided easily that they were sisters. "What did you say to him?" she asked her husband. "When he said that, what'd you say?"

Kip's eyes stayed on the car in front of them. "I don't know," he said. "He was like, 'you little faggot,' and I said, 'I'm waiting for my wife and kid, how am I a faggot?'" Without looking, Kip could feel their four eyes on him. The silence in the car deepened. "What?" he said grumpily.

"You said that?" Denny said.

"I—" Kip started. Joanna looked at him in that pitying, patronizing way she had. "You weren't there," he said to her. "So stop with the look. In fact, neither of you was there, and that's why this thing happened in the first place."

Joanna exhaled and shook her head slowly.

Kip said, "Den, come on, you saw him. The guy is enormous and clearly everyone is on edge here. Joanna, you just said we don't want to invite danger. What was I supposed to say?"

"Not that," Joanna said.

"Explain to me what I said that was so wrong," Kip said, irritated, his mind swimming, unable to get a hold of anything solid.

Once again Joanna got out of the car and began walking up the road. Kip watched her disappear past the cars in front of them.

"Kiddo," he said to Denny. "I'm not excusing that kind of language."

But his son had already put on his headphones and turned his eyes downward and Kip's words went unheard.

. . . .

It wasn't that Kip was stupid, Joanna thought. He wasn't. He had his own forms of intelligence. He was very good at math, for instance. He could calculate a tip like it was nothing. But she had to admit that this talent didn't quite make up for something she'd always felt he lacked. It was like he was never quite fully present, his eyes going just slightly blank whenever a topic of any seriousness came up, and when you're never fully present, it makes it hard to understand the things happening around you. She hated reductive bumper-sticker slogans like "If you aren't pissed off, you aren't paying attention," but, well, that one wasn't wrong. His desire was for everyone—most especially her and Denny— to be happy and comfortable, and that was admirable, but she couldn't help but feel that to achieve this he turned away from the things in life that needed to be met head-on. Just once she would have liked to get into the car after him and find the radio tuned to NPR rather than one of his music channels—"First Wave" or "Deep Vinyl"—to know that for once he was looking up, looking around, listening, paying attention to anything really happening in the world. Didn't he see the struggles Denny had in school? Didn't he see how hard it was for the boy, even in this so-called more enlightened time when kids were questioning the constructs of gender and accepting each other? Didn't it ever even occur to him that some things couldn't be solved with a "Hey, buddy," and a hair mussing?

She made her way between the cars, reverse-prayering her arms, focusing on the simple stretch, her chest widening, opening up her breathing.

No, Kip wasn't stupid. He was kind and caring, and he would do anything for her and Denny. But he was also clueless in a way that few people could afford to be anymore, and Joanna had to admit that she resented him for this. It wasn't regret she felt when she came back and endured his speeches about her drinking and getting the whole family to spend more time outdoors—as if he'd ever hiked a trail in his life—and generally getting them all back "on the right foot." For it had been her to leave. It had been her who left her family for a six-month midlife walkabout in Austin, Skyping with her clients and Facetiming with Denny and spending evenings drinking at galleries and rock shows until she felt her thoughts getting muddled, heard her speech betraying her inebriation, and then coming back to her shitty furnished apartment to finish the job by herself like a good, responsible drunk. These were her decisions, her actions, and if she had to now sit on their bed and listen to him talk about the benefits of being around trees, then so be it. No, it wasn't regret she felt those first weeks. But rather a deep, saturating resignation.

That is, until Kirsten.

• • • •

Kip was angry when she returned. He stared straight ahead, his mouth pulled tight. Traffic had moved again while Joanna was out—not far, fifty yards or so, but enough for him to feel anxious and then righteous in his anger. Couldn't she stay put? Couldn't she just sit there like he did instead of walking off down the damn highway? And why did he feel like he was on the defensive, as if he'd done something wrong? He was right there. Always, always, he was right there.

"Well, I'm glad I didn't have to drive off and leave you behind," he said. "I'll tell you one thing, I'm not getting my butt kicked by that redneck back there because you want to stretch your legs."

"You would have passed me, Kip," she had said, so calmly, as if had she just taken a stroll around the block back home. It was infuriating.

"Or you could get hit by a car."

"What'd you get up to, five miles an hour?"

"I'm trying to get my family clear of a goddamn tropical storm," he said, his voice raised, urgent. "That's all I want to do right now."

Denny took his headphones off.

"So do I," Joanna said. "I packed up just as much—"

"No, you want to have some kind of existential crisis every twenty minutes," Kip said. He was nearly shouting now, or as close to shouting as he got. "You want to find out what the storm *means*. But it doesn't mean anything. You just have to get out of its way."

In his periphery, he saw his wife watching him. That look again.

"Fine!" Kip snapped. "Fine! Forget it."

"Why are you so upset?" Joanna said.

"I'm not," Kip said, shrugging. "I'm not. I'm just . . . I'll tell you what. I'm going for a walk now. How's that?"

"It's fine."

"It's my turn," he said. "My turn to go walk on the highway! Why not!"

"Dad?" Denny said.

"I'll be back, buddy." He shut the door and stomped off between the lane and the crowded shoulder.

Joanna breathed and spun in her seat to face Denny. Through the back window she could see the sky over the city growing blacker.

"He's fine," she told her son.

"Why's he so mad?"

"He's mad at me," Joanna said.

Denny turned from her gaze, directing his eyes to the sisters in the Prius. "Mom," he said. "What does 'I've got the itch' mean?" His heart was racing, and the skin on the backs of his hands went cold.

Joanna didn't say anything for a moment. "I guess it depends on the context," she said finally. "What are you talking about?"

"I've got the itch, baby," he said.

Joanna closed her eyes, felt her life slipping down into a dark hole.

Denny said, "Do you have a boyfriend or something?"

"Something like that," she said.

"Are you going to leave again?"

Joanna's lip quivered. "You know, you're the reason I came back," she said. "Do you know that? Do you know how much I love you?"

"So are you?"

"I don't know," she said, though this was a lie. They both knew it.

"What if he doesn't take you back this time?"

"I wouldn't ask him to," she said.

Denny sighed. "Well, he probably would, anyway. He's nicer than you."

Joanna wiped her nose with a sleeve. "Yeah, I guess he probably is," she said. "But I wouldn't ask." She trained her eyes on the sky out the sunroof, trying to keep gravity from working any more on her tears. Right above them it was blue and cloudless. "It isn't a boyfriend," she said. "It's a woman."

"Oh," Denny said. With this his feelings of betrayal morphed into something else, something harder to pin down. He felt a little bit sorry for his mom. It must have been hard for her. People like his parents didn't know how to be themselves. Not that being himself was always easy, especially in high school, but school wouldn't last forever. In a few years he would be done with all that. People like his parents, though, they were stuck. They were like their own high schools.

"What's her name?" he asked.

"Kirsten," she said. How strange it felt to say her name out loud, to her son. She realized that she hadn't had a reason to say it to anyone aside from Kirsten herself.

Denny said, "Does Dad know?"

"No. He doesn't."

"Are you going to tell him?"

"Yes."

"I didn't know you . . ." Denny's words trailed off.

"I didn't know either," Joanna said. "Does it make a difference?"

"No," Denny said. "I don't know. Yeah, I guess so. I guess maybe it must be real or else you wouldn't go through it."

Joanna forced her mouth into a smile while inside her heart broke for all the ways she'd failed her son.

"It'll be worse for Dad, though," Denny said. "He won't understand. It won't, like, compute."

Joanna knew he was right. But what Denny didn't know, what Joanna couldn't say to him, was that Kip wouldn't understand because he wouldn't allow himself to understand. He wouldn't try. He wouldn't want to. He would find anger and victimhood and hang onto those for a long, long time. And in some ways he would be right. Joanna would be the one to leave, and she would have to learn to live with being the bad guy.

"You can come with me," she said. "I can stay in the district so you wouldn't have to change schools."

"I hate my school," Denny said. "But I doubt anywhere else is any better. Anyway, I need to stay with Dad."

Tears fell from Joanna's eyes. "No," she managed to say. "You don't. That's not your job."

But he would. This was something he'd inherited from his father. Family first, always. And when Denny officially comes out to Kip—without a doubt before he does to Joanna—Kip will be honestly surprised, and he'll take an almost imperceptible moment for his confusion before refocusing on his child, still his child, and taking that thin body in his arms.

Just then the brake lights on the VW in front of them came on, and Joanna heard engines all around turn over. "Shit," she said. The VW started to pull away. The big guy in the Charger was leaning forward onto the steering wheel. Joanna origami'd herself into the driver's seat and turned the car on. "Do you see him?" she said, trying to keep her voice calm but admitting to herself that she did feel that anxiety Kip had complained about. She put the car in drive and nervously began to inch forward.

Denny slid the window down and put his head out into the hot, humid air and looked each way, back toward the city and ahead to the flat expanse of eastern Texas, and sure enough there he was, Kip, Denny's father, jogging toward them between the creeping cars, a smile of relief alighting on his face when his eyes met with his son's. He slowed to a walk, raising a hand and waving. Joanna came to a stop, and Kip was in the passenger seat a moment before traffic really started to pick up—fifteen, twenty, thirty miles per hour. Breathless and relieved, Kip said, "You see? You see why we have to stick together?"

COORDINATED EFFORTS

. . . .

A thud from somewhere in the house launched me from my bed, my heart rattling wildly in my chest. Next to me, Michaela still slept. My phone, on the bedside table, read 6:13 a.m. and only nine percent battery. I listened a moment and heard nothing, then took the bat I'd been keeping under the bed and went out to the hall, but all I found was our daughter, Amelia, already dressed, trying to read by the dim dawn light coming through her bedroom window.

"I couldn't sleep," she said.

"Did you drop a book or something?" I asked.

"Sorry," she said.

Sorry? I wanted to say. *Kid, you scared the shit out of me.* The city was in a state since the storm—well, since the election, really, but even more so since the storm—and everyone, myself included, was on edge. Not without reason. Things had been happening. Break-ins. Attacks. Protests and counterprotests. The world was a place I couldn't understand anymore.

I said to my daughter, "You hungry?"

"Yes," she said. "Is there any milk for cereal?"

"If there is, it's gone bad by now," I said. "Give me five minutes. We'll go out. I need to charge my phone somewhere anyway."

The power had been out in our neighborhood for two weeks at that point, ever since a tropical storm crashed into the coast, just thirty miles from us. The rest of the city had lights after just a few days. *Problems with transformers* was the reason given for our delayed illumination, but rumors were spreading about this being part of a plan. Things like this had been happening in other cities that had mayors in cahoots with our new would-be Supreme Leader. Gay neighborhoods, Hispanic neighborhoods, artsy liberal enclaves like ours. They all seemed to be enduring increasing neglect. Sewers backed up. 911 slower to respond. Road repairs all but ceased. A coordinated assault of pettiness coming down from the new on high.

I took Michaela's phone to charge it too. The eastern sky was brightening from purple to blue by the time we got outside. The rains had continued periodically since the big storm, and the old uneven sidewalks of our neighborhood were full of puddles. Amelia wore her rubber boots and a pullover hoodie. She was just seven, but how grown up she looked. You could already start to see the woman she would be.

There was a bakery not far past the edge of the blackout zone that we had been to once or twice before. It was only a half-dozen blocks away, but the differences between the neighborhoods were obvious. The brick colonials and craftsmans of our area were replaced by thousand-square-foot shotguns with tiny front yards demarcated by chain-link fences. Where our street boasted a canopy of oaks and elms, over here there were almost no trees to offset the endless lines of cars parked at the curbs.

There was no one else at the bakery yet, just us and the girl at the counter. I ordered a few bagels and a coffee, then realized I'd neglected to bring a phone charger. "You wouldn't happen to have an iPhone charger, would you?" I asked the girl.

"Yeah, no problem," the girl said. I checked Michaela's phone, which was still at thirty-six percent. The girl unplugged her phone from a cord by the coffee machine, and I handed her mine.

"I appreciate it," I told her.

We sat near the window. I tried not to glance at the girl behind the counter, though it was difficult. She was young, twenty or twenty-one, with icy blue eyes, round cheeks, and a smile that, when it appeared, took over the whole of her face. A luminous human being, she was. And I thought, some guy or girl out there gets to wake up to this person in the morning, gets to smell the soap on her skin after she showers, gets to set dinner down in front of her. I had no doubt that people had thought the same about Michaela, that they still did, but this only went so far to relieve me of the desire to be all people at once. Our existences were so tragically singular, our vision so limited, our experiences so piddly. That we claimed to know anything was the biggest sham of all.

The girl looked over and caught one of my glances. Smiled. Christ, what a face. She said, "You all in the blackout zone?"

"How'd you guess?" I said.

"Our outlets are pretty popular," she said.

"I bet," I said.

"Work at the university?"

"I do," I said. "I'm a professor." I was trying to impress her, I admit. "Are you a student?"

"I was. I graduated this past semester."

"Congratulations."

"First generation college graduate," she said.

"Is that right? Good for you. Well done."

The girl pursed her lips into something akin to a grin, though it never quite made it there.

"You look like a professor," she said.

"Do I?"

I was honestly surprised by this. Since everything started—before the storm and the blackout, even before the new administration, back when the change was little more than a slightly more vocal outrage in the cultural ether—I'd altered my look a bit, tried to tone down the

39

professorial touches. I shaved my beard and had Michaela trim my hair. I stopped wearing so much brown and started with more blues and grays. I left at home the *New Yorker* tote bag I normally used to bring my lunch to campus, opting instead for a reusable bag from the grocery. I started crossing my legs at the ankle rather than the knee. Stupid, I know, but this is what things had devolved into.

"I'm sure it'll get figured out soon," the girl said. "The power and all."

"Yeah, I hope so."

"And then everyone can get back to their charmed lives."

A bit of bagel lodged in my throat. I drank from my coffee, and it burned my mouth. "I'm not sure I would call my life charmed," I said.

The girl shrugged and tapped at her phone and would not look my way. "Lucky?" she said. "Elite? Whatever. You know what I mean."

"Dad?" Amelia said.

"Hang on, hon," I said, continuing to watch the girl. "I'm not sure I do know," I told her.

"My grandfather was a bricklayer," she said.

I waited for more. "And mine was a grocer in Sacramento," I said. The political blatherings about the rise of the Real America were near constant, but to hear it from young people was always particularly demoralizing. They were supposed to be the ones who could see through all of that, but even they had started to buy in.

"I think I know what you're getting at," I said. "But if I may ask, what is it you think you know about us and our lives?"

"It's nothing to get upset about. It's just that people like you have been running this country for a good long time."

"People like me," I said.

"Yeah," she said, shrugging again. "And look where it's gotten us. So now it's our turn."

My stomach roiled, the coffee in it going sour. I stood, said, "Come on, sweetheart," to Amelia. She hadn't finished her food. I pulled a couple of napkins from a dispenser and wrapped what was left, put it in my pocket. At the door I turned to the girl. "Tell your bosses you lost them a customer."

"Oh no," she said shittily.

· · · ·

Just after the election, I was attacked. I'd come to work late that day after a dentist appointment, and all of the spots in my usual parking lot were taken, and so I was forced to park on the street in the neighborhood adjacent to campus. I had an evening class, and it was dark by the time I left. Two young men stood smoking cigarettes. I passed them by, and just as I realized they were following me, one of them tagged me in the ribs. For an interminable moment, even after I took a shot to the head, I didn't really understand what was happening. *You're punching me*, I wanted to tell them, as if this was all a big misunderstanding. But then I got a nasty pop to the jaw and the sidewalk jumped up to slam me in the side and I was taking boots to my ribs and back. It lasted only a minute, maybe less, but that was enough to put me in the hospital for a day and a half.

I don't think the two men were waiting for me. I don't think it was personal. They saw an opportunity and took it. I think they were making a point, and it was the same point the girl at the bakery wanted to make. *You don't make the rules anymore.*

· · · ·

Amelia and I found Michaela up and making coffee in our French press. Thankfully we had a gas range and could still cook food and boil water. Amelia shuffled off to the living room with a book and, alone now, I told Michaela about the girl at the bakery.

"God," she said. "What'd you say?"

"That I wasn't going to buy my bagels there anymore."

"Told her," she said.

"Yeah, she was very upset."

I checked on Amelia on the couch. I had to admit that the whole nonsense with the power outage had had a benefit: our daughter was reading more. No tv, no tablets, no games. And after a few days she'd stopped complaining. I think at that point I missed my limitless flashing screen more than she did.

"Was that girl being mean to you?" Amelia asked.

"At the bakery? She wasn't being particularly pleasant," I said.

"Why?"

Why. People were being attacked verbally and physically. Vandals had taken to the streets with seeming impunity. Five professors at my university had received death threats for crimes ranging from being Muslim to not calling on people in the right order. I got the shit beat out of me. But according to people on all sides, it was up to *us* to understand. On the question of why, I wavered between *Yes, I want to know* and *Fuck you and everyone like you.*

"I'm not sure, hon," I told my daughter. "You ever wake up grumpy?"

"No," she said.

"Fibber," I said, and she laughed.

Michaela came in from the kitchen, said, "Have you seen my phone?"

"Yeah, I was going to charge it," I said, just a half-moment before shame and regret toppled me. "Oh fuck me," I muttered. My phone was still behind the counter at the bakery.

I sat with Amelia on the couch, let my head fall back.

"Are you going to go get it?" Michaela asked.

"I'll go this afternoon."

"After the girl's shift?"

I looked over at her. "Yeah," I said.

Michaela sat on the arm of the couch and put her fingers through my hair. "It wasn't her that jumped you, Peter."

"Yeah, I know it wasn't her. Jesus."

"She's just some girl at a bakery."

"I know that." Michaela tilted her head and gave me a look that said *Do you?* "I *know that,*" I said.

Michaela stood and tapped and swiped at her phone. "Oh geez," she said. Amelia and I both looked up. "Jeff and Susi's roof collapsed last night in the rain," Michaela said. "The living room is soaked." Jeff and Susi were friends in the neighborhood. Susi worked at the university— women's and gender studies—and Jeff was a sculptor.

"That's a bummer," I said. "Are they able to get anyone in today to look at it?"

"They're trying, but everyone is booked since the storm. The thing is that they were supposed to host the thing tonight."

Just after the storm, people in the neighborhood had begun holding get-togethers with musicians, acting troupes, performers of all stripes, mostly to pool the entertainment resources and while away the darker hours. Candles were bought and lit, and the shows commenced. Michaela and I had been to a few of these "performance parties," as people had begun to call them: an opera singer on Marshall Street, an original theater piece on Telford. The performances were always followed by conversations that would inevitably veer toward the current political crisis, with opinions varying from *This is democracy's death knell* to *This is the whole goddamn world's death knell.* Everyone nodded and shook their heads as appropriate. And yet there we were in the candlelight, listening to music, drinking wine, eating brie and dark chocolates with sea salt. Was it possible we didn't really believe our own dire prognoses? Or did we feel so helpless that we figured we might as well have some snacks while we watched everything we cared about in this life become devalued and everything we loathed deregulated? After the lights came back on elsewhere in the city, the parties continued to be held in our neighborhood, and they'd taken on more significance. They were symbols of resilience and resistance. And if our resistance came with Bach and Beckett, well, no one said the handbasket we all went to hell in couldn't be a well-appointed one.

"Is it canceled then?" I asked Michaela.

"No," she said, "Susi's asking if we can host."

· · · ·

I went full Dalloway and told Michaela I would buy the flowers myself. She said, "Yeah, you're going to do a lot more than that." We would have our work cut out for us, since we'd let the place go somewhat in the weeks since the storm. We had to clean the kitchen, the bathrooms. Finally fold and put away the laundry we'd done at the laundromat three days before. Get candles and booze and snacks. Vacuuming was not an option, so we rolled up the rugs and brought them outside, hung them over a railing and let Amelia go wild beating them with a broom, which she seemed to enjoy.

The performers would be a violin quartet, though we did not know what music they were planning. It didn't really matter. The gathering was the thing, not necessarily the playing. We moved the couch and arranged some folding chairs from the basement along the walls. Pushed the dining room table out of the center of the room and set it up for grazing.

I made PB-and-Js for lunch, and then Michaela said, "So, you're going out?" I hung my head, then got up and grabbed my keys.

I had to go to three different Targets to find enough candles and batteries. At each one, the cashier said, "Blackout zone?" and I said, "Yep." And that was it.

After getting the wine and food, there was nothing else for me to do but go back to the bakery for my phone. I hated the fact that my scalp went hot with anxiety at the chance I might see the girl again. I parked and stepped with feigned confidence into the shop. No girl. Behind the counter was a man, older than me by at least twenty-five, maybe thirty years. This I could deal with.

I told him I'd left my phone earlier; was there one behind the counter? The old baker pivoted in place, pushed a couple of loaves around on the counter behind him.

"Don't see one," he said. His voice was deep and phlegmy.

"Not by the coffee machine?"

He looked. "Nope," he said. "Let me check in back."

A few more people came in and gazed into the glass cases full of pastries and cookies and sweets I couldn't name. The old baker came back out. "Sorry," he said.

Anger surged through me. She stole my phone. It was just a phone, ok, but she stole it, and worse, she stole it because she felt it was her *right* to steal it.

The old baker turned to the others and asked them what he could do for them.

"Sorry," I said, interrupting. "Sorry, but we're going to need to figure this out." I told him in more detail what had transpired: the phone charger, the girl taking my phone in her hand. A level of trust, I said. "And I didn't want to mention this, but she was quite rude to my daughter and me."

"Oh," the old baker said. I tried to pretend I didn't feel the other customers watching me. "All right," he said. "Let's see what's going on." He stepped into the back room once again.

I turned to the other customers. "Sorry," I said. They turned away, back to the sweets case.

. . . .

The baker gave me a cup of coffee while we waited, but it only soured my stomach. He'd used an old cordless landline to call the girl, and I watched him stride back and forth through the swinging door between the kitchen and the front of the shop as she directed him where to look. *Find it*, my useless internal pleading repeated, but I knew that he wouldn't.

"She says it's here," he told me. "But I don't know. She's coming in."

I nodded and kept nodding too long. "Great," I said finally.

"These phones," he said. "They got people's whole lives on them, huh."

"Yeah," I said.

"Some people, it's like losing an arm."

"It's mostly my work stuff," I said.

"Sure, sure," he said.

After twenty minutes, the girl arrived. Out from behind the counter, I saw the length of her for the first time. She wore jeans torn at the knees and a t-shirt that proclaimed her allegiance to the new administration.

"Thanks for coming back in, sweetie," the old baker said to her.

"No big deal." She did not look at me at my table in the corner, the same one I'd sat at with Amelia earlier. She went behind the counter and through the swinging door, only to come back out a moment later with my phone in her hand.

"Where was it?" the old baker asked.

"Right where I said it was," the girl said with mock exasperation.

"My eyes," he said, shaking his head. "My brain."

She came to me and handed me the phone. "There you go," she said.

"Thank you."

I thanked the old baker and then, against my better judgment (which, as always, took the form of Michaela's voice in my head, saying *Don't do it, baby*) I followed the girl out the door.

"Excuse me," I said to her back. She turned. "I just thought," I said. What did I just think? "I wanted to talk to you."

"Ok."

"I don't know what I personally did to offend you."

"Nothing," she said. "I don't know you."

"But you think you do, don't you? Enough to say what you said."

She slumped her shoulders forward. "It was just a comment," she said. "You probably have a good life. Would you say you have a good life?"

"Sure," I said.

"Ok then."

"But that doesn't mean anything," I said.

"It might not mean anything to you. I know a lot of people who would appreciate a little more comfort in their lives."

"That's not what I meant."

"I know what you meant," she said. "You want us to keep watching you elites give this country's resources to immigrants and welfare queens while we lose our jobs and our homes. Well, we're not going to anymore. I'm not going to work at a bakery for the rest of my life—"

"No one is asking you to."

"—while you stand in front of a classroom and tell everyone how the world works and why we should all give in to your agenda."

"That doesn't make sense," I said.

"I guess it's up to you to say what makes sense."

Her calmness was increasingly frustrating, and I found myself losing touch with any point I might have had a moment before. "No," I said.

"Look," she said. "It's been really great talking to you. But I have places to be. I'll be sure to come see you during office hours so you can explain the world to me some more." She stepped to an old Camry and opened the door. I watched in silence, my mind swimming like I'd just gotten clocked in the face. The passenger side window was open, and as she pulled away from the curb, I heard her say, "Have fun at your party tonight."

. . . .

"We're not canceling," Michaela said.

She was mopping the hardwoods in the entryway. She'd already dusted the bookshelves and opened the windows to air the place out while I was gone. Amelia was in her room.

"This girl is nuts, hon," I said.

"I don't care. I already told Susi we would do it, and she already sent the Facebook thing around. We're not changing locations again." I followed her to the kitchen and washed the lunch dishes. "So she read your email," Michaela said. "She's a stupid kid. She's got no manners. That doesn't mean she's going to do anything."

"Who knows what information she got."

"Change all your passwords, first off," she said. "And put a security code on your phone. I've told you to do that before."

"That's hardly the point," I said.

Michaela shrugged. She went back to the living room but returned a moment later. "Shit," she said. "You could have gotten some cookies for tonight while you were there."

. . . .

People started to arrive at seven, entering our house in pairs and trios. I shook hands and took coats to the guest bedroom. The few children in tow made their way to Amelia's room, where they formed a fete of their own. By eight her room looked like it had been tossed by a team of determined burglars.

Michaela and I poured wine and popped beers. We refilled chip bowls and un-cellophaned plates handed to us by our guests. As the sun settled below the western edge of the neighborhood, we lit more candles until the whole house glowed yellow-orange. I attempted to make pleasant chitchat, but I couldn't help keeping an eye, and a good part of my mind, on the street out front. I kept imagining the girl from the bakery showing up like Arnold Friend, leaning against that Camry of hers, flanked by some gang of all-Americans intent on retribution against us effete liberals for ignoring them all these years. Ready to tear us all apart.

Right around nine, we cleared a space in the living room, and the performance began. I supposed I'd expected something rather serene, a nice Schumann or Mozart, maybe even a bit of Vivaldi for a crowd-pleaser. What I hadn't expected was the melancholy and occasionally sinister minimalism of John Cage. The long near-silences of the piece were interrupted by discordant shrieks of bow and string that made my shoulders tense, as if someone was breathing too close behind me. I glanced out the front window. A car drove by, slowly. I couldn't make out the model.

The quartet continued for nearly a half hour, during which time I increasingly felt as if I were balancing on the precipice of a heart attack. The notes seemed to infiltrate my chest and muddy my mind. My vision blurred. The temperature in the room rose, and sweat trickled down my face. The men who attacked me alighted in my consciousness, but rather than lurking silently as they normally did, now they screamed, their half-formed, shadowed faces contorted and crimson with rage against me, against my family, against everyone in my house that night. They were all I could see, all I could hear. And I knew that their screams were the soundtrack of the world now. Our new national anthem.

By the time the musicians finished, my shirt was damp and I felt as if I might drop, exhausted from the effort of staving off a full fit of hysterical dread. I clapped lightly along with the rest of the neighbors crowding my house. A couple men called for an encore, and I thought *Oh, god, please no*. Thankfully, the quartet did not give in. They did, however, accept the wine Michaela brought them, and glasses were raised to another delightful gathering.

A while later I stood on the porch, thanking people for coming. The air felt almost cold against my sweat-slicked skin. The stream of people slowed and then stopped, and I peered inside to find our candle-lit house empty save for my family. I could hear Michaela in the kitchen cleaning up. Amelia was asleep upstairs. I let the screen door ease it-self shut and sat on the steps of the porch. The dark and quiet of our neighborhood felt somehow profound. I imagined a plane flying over-head, the passengers looking down and finding a small black dot in the middle of our bright city. That was us.

I took my phone from my pocket and found a text message on the screen. *How's the party, professor?*

I read it again and again, feeling violated, as if she'd slipped into our house and messed with our things.

Who is this? I texted back, though of course I knew.

A minute passed before the reply came. *Keira*, it read.

I was in the process of replying, firmly telling her to never contact me again, when she wrote, *Meet me at the bakery*.

What made me even consider it? This girl, a stranger outside of two hostile encounters, could have had anything waiting for me. Friends ready to pound me into the ground with pipes and bats and fists. A camera rolling, ready to capture me in some out-of-context moment, fuel for a blackmail scheme. I had no idea, and yet I didn't say no. Some part of me wanted all of this to happen. I didn't want another beating, of course, but I would take it to prove a point. I wanted to put my morality up against their anger and watch their bigoted wall of self-righteous self-pity crumble with every punch and kick I absorbed.

My fingers shook as I texted back. *15 mins.*

I told Michaela I was going out for a drive, needed to clear my head, it had been a long day, a long week, ever since the storm, ever since the election, just craziness, you know what I mean?

"I guess," she said. "Text me if you're going to be late."

There was no one in the bakery's front lot. I clicked my door locks down and pulled into the side lot. The headlights found her standing at the rear entry door, seemingly alone. I pulled up and pressed the window down a few inches.

"I'm not gonna bite," she said. She took a pack of Marlboros from her small purse and lit one. "You want?"

"No," I said, rolling the window down the rest of the way. She was still wearing the shirt she'd been in earlier. American flag and he-who-shall-not-be-named's name emblazoned over her lovely breasts. "What can I do for you?" I said.

"I was kind of a dickhead today."

"You read my emails."

"Yeah," she said. "I did. I shouldn't have."

"Was the phone really here when I came back, when your boss couldn't find it?"

"That actually was an accident," she said. "I must have put it in my pocket to get it out of the way or something and then forgot about it. I wasn't, like, stealing it. I'm not a thief."

She took a misstep backward, catching herself with a hand against the bakery wall.

"Are you drunk?" I said.

"Not *drunk*," she said. "But, yeah, a little." She took a drag on her cigarette. "Do you think you could give me a ride home?"

"Are you fucking kidding me?"

51

"My car is here, so if you think I should be driving right now, then I'll trust your judgment, professor."

In that moment my anger toward her gave way to concern I felt toward my students: a protectiveness, a desire to see them safe and successful.

"Put the cigarette out and get in," I said.

She told me where she lived—just two, maybe three miles away, in the direction opposite my neighborhood.

"Why'd you text me?" I asked her. "Why not a friend?"

"I wanted to apologize."

"And you needed a ride."

"Two birds," she said with a shrug. "Plus I figured it would freak you out a little."

She watched out the window as I took a turn, then another. It was a desolate night, no one out.

"So how was your party?" she said.

"It was fine," I said, then thought about it. "Actually, it was awful. I spent most of the time having a fucking panic attack."

"My mom has those."

"I got jumped a while ago," I told her. "A couple guys not far from the university. Just started hitting me, kicking me. Broke two ribs. My face isn't even healed all the way. In the light you can still see the bruises."

"That sucks," she said.

"It sucks," I agreed. "And those are your people. That's who you've aligned yourself with."

"Fuck that. Don't put that on me. I don't know those dudes."

"You'll understand someday," I said. "At least I hope you do."

"Condescend much?" she said.

We drove on in silence. I felt helpless, useless. This, I supposed, was what drove people insane: the unfathomable chasms between us all. The budding knowledge that what we are is all we will ever be.

Keira tapped at her phone, and then mine rattled its bed of coins in the center console.

Pull over, it read.

"Here?" I said.

She didn't look up from her phone. Mine buzzed in my hand.

Yes here

I pulled to the curb, waited for her to get out or say something, but she only continued to thumb her phone's screen.

Kiss me

My heart lurched and blood rushed to my cock. "No," I said.

You want to

Of course I did. Despite her ignorant, repugnant view of the world, there was only one reason I was there—to kiss her. Or maybe in some perverse way it was exactly because of her views. I'd never put myself into a position like this before. So why now? Why her?

"It'll be our secret," she said in a teasing whisper. "I'm moving away in a couple weeks anyway. You'll never even see me again."

Despite the dim light, her face glowed, seemed incandescent. So beautiful. I thought of the friends and colleagues with whom I'd spent the evening, thought of them seeing me with this girl in that shirt, them witnessing this horrible, intoxicating transgression. I would be shunned, ostracized. The thought only urged me on.

Hating myself but unable to resist, I leaned toward her, my heart thumping wildly. Our lips touched and, after a moment, her tongue emerged from the cave of her mouth to moisten our connection. I could taste whatever rotgut booze she'd drunk earlier, and I was sure she could taste my half-decent wine. My hand went to her side, and I felt her breathing under the rolling waves of her ribs. I wanted to consume the girl, wanted her to consume me. I wanted us to dissolve into particles and become something new together. It was the most desperate of hungers, the impossibility of its satisfaction only serving to intensify the desire. Yes, this is what drives people insane.

Her lips closed around my tongue and then she pulled back, as though getting the last bits of something sweet off a spoon. She sighed heavily and then opened the door. "Catch you later," she said with a grin.

I said nothing, afraid that words would wash the taste of her from my mouth.

Before shutting the door, she leaned back in. "See," she said. "You're no better than us."

· · · ·

The lights came on the next day. Michaela, Amelia, and I came home from a trip to the mall, none of us noticing for a few minutes that a lamp in the corner was on, just as it had been when the electric went out three weeks before. We raised our arms and cheered, then celebrated by going to the grocery store and stocking the fridge and freezer with all manner of perishables. That evening we watched a movie together, eating popcorn hot from the microwave. Through the celebration, just below the veil of my demeanor, I was sick with guilt, not just for betraying my wife and our vows—though that would have been enough—but for what seemed to be a betrayal of decency and conscience. I'd fortified the girl's beliefs, and that made me feel like I'd let the whole world down. I'd been deplorable. And worse yet, along with the guilt twisting in my gut, there was the memory of those few moments in the car, those measly seconds when our mouths mingled, and the memory of how good it felt, how easy and simple and *good* it felt to think of only myself, my immediate desire for her, and if there was anything positive to come from my transgression, it might have been that I understood the world a tiny bit better.

Michaela stayed up late reading in bed, taking advantage of the fact that she could. I closed my eyes but did not fall asleep for a good long while. All I wanted to do was drive Keira from my thoughts, an impossible task. But as insistent as her presence was in my mind, there was also something else, another memory clip playing simultaneously. Back on the night of the storm, Michaela and I had stood in our doorway, watching the deluge through the screen door. It was past ten and Amelia was asleep on the couch, her fatigue finally winning out over the excitement and anxiety of the weather. As the storm peaked, transformers throughout the neighborhood blew, booming and sending flashes of green over the houses. I put my arm around my wife's waist, and she leaned into my shoulder. The closest explosion yet sounded and we both jumped and our entire street went black.

"I guess that's that," Michaela said. "We should light some candles." But neither of us moved, instead remaining there in the doorway for another minute or more, listening to the rush of the storm, unable to quite make out the rain crashing down in the darkness.

HOW TO BE FREE

· · · ·

A placard at the conference room door reads "No Electronic Devices or Firearms." Enter and find more than half of the hundred or so seats empty. Of the people there, few sit in pairs. Most leave some distance between each other, two or three seats at least. Take a chair at the end of a row and watch people shuffle in with their heads down, many with hands held over their faces. A half dozen have on Guy Fawkes masks. Even more wear lightweight scarves up over their mouths and noses. Lord, what must be happening to them? Worry that you haven't used enough caution on this trip. You've read of people with whole aliases complete with IDs and even birth certificates, but you aren't there yet. You did cancel your credit cards—an act that annoyed your husband Martin to no end—and you have a handful of email addresses for different purposes and a disposable cell phone. In the grand scheme, though, this is amateur-hour stuff.

What little chatter floats through the room quiets to silence as a door at the front opens and a woman strides in. She wears a black dress and an auburn pixie cut. Not that these are the aspects any person on the street would notice. No, they would notice the mask. A sort of cross between a medical mask and a Wild West bandit's kerchief, it appears at first to likewise be black, but as the woman walks toward the crowd, you see that it is actually a lovely deep purple.

Mask or no mask, you know who she is. Gloria Downing. Not her real name, of course, but the name she took on as her role in the movement became more prominent. When first hearing of her, you thought that perhaps she was British. That was the only other place you'd ever heard the word. Downing Street. But by now you've listened to dozens of hours of the woman's voice on YouTube, and there is no doubting her Americanness. She might be midwestern, given the absence of any other telling geographical accent. Like a mainstream media anchorwoman. She could even be from Omaha, your home—wouldn't that be something. Or perhaps, you think now, she shed an accent she had earlier in life, all the better to cloak herself.

Gloria Downing looks out at the people in the room, and then she speaks, her voice clear and loud and unrushed. Listen.

"You're a good person. You know right from wrong, and you try to do right. You do not break the law. You do not violate the codes of conduct that keep society from falling into chaos. You mow your lawn. You pay the electric. You had a good family growing up, or maybe you didn't. Maybe you endured abuse and neglect. Maybe you went to school, achieved academic success. Or maybe you went to work, tried your best to earn an honest living. You are a good person. But what has been happening to you is not what a good person deserves. You lost your job. You got kicked out of school. You got sick. You lost your wife, your husband. Your child. Or you were never able to find that right person to start a family with in the first place. You're scared to go outside. You're scared to use the phone, the computer, to turn on the tv. To drive a car, to get on an airplane. You can't sleep. You are lonely. But you are not alone. No one believes you? Baloney. I believe you. Everyone in this room believes you. People say you are crazy, but let me tell you something: you are not crazy. You have been targeted."

Sit transfixed. You've forgotten the fatigue, the jet lag, even the hunger (you've had nothing all day but pretzels and ginger ale on the plane). So rapt is your attention on the woman at the front of the room.

As Gloria Downing continues, the other people in the room sit erect, though a few have gone the other way, crumpling forward into themselves, hands over their mouths. You get it. Someone is speaking to them, truly speaking to them. Someone understands everything they've been through, are still going through. The pain. The fear. It's overwhelming. Her words penetrate and find some roiling magma long buried and denied. Hope. Allow yourself this.

• • • •

Sit through three more speakers after Gloria Downing, all men, each of them telling their own stories of organized harassment and how they are working, with the help of the Coalition of Targeted Individuals, to uncover the foe or foes behind their harassment, or, barring discovery, to at least live within the confines of their situation. Notice that no one has actually found their tormentors, but appreciate that they were here, trying to help others, living despite it all. You have been thinking more and more that you cannot. Cannot keep living.

After the presentations, stand at a table where they are selling Gloria Downing's new book, *Let It Be Known: A Guidebook for Targeted Individuals*.

"Did you read the other one?" a voice sounds behind. A short, girthy black man. He seems to be the only person of color in the crowd. He holds a copy of Gloria's first book, *In the Shadows, Not in the Dark*. "Chapter nine," he says. "Me. Like she was talking to me."

Purse your lips into a faint smile. You thought about bringing the book, too—it's upstairs in your suitcase—and asking for an autograph, but didn't want to appear frivolous or sycophantic.

"You read it?" the man says. "She talks about the early technologies. That's something we forget about. We think this all started with computers and the internet and whatnot. But back at the beginning they were getting to me through my radio. In my house, in my car. Listening in. It goes back a long ways, all this. We aren't the first generation, and we won't be the last."

"I hope you're wrong," you say. "About being the last. God willing, we'll uncover something. Someone will. Maybe we could be the last ones."

"Amen," the man says. He claps the book against his palm. "I go by Larry," he says.

"Tamara," you say.

His eyebrows rise. "I got a sister named Tamara," he says, but as soon as the words flee his mouth, his face falls. You understand. You did the same thing, revealed yourself, gave away something true to a person you do not know. There is a sense of safety in this room, especially after Gloria's speech, and if the other people there are anything like you, they want so badly to be open, unguarded.

Tell him, "It's ok. I'm not one of them."

But you both know that this is exactly what one of them would say.

• • • •

In the room upstairs, think about what the man called Larry said about being surveilled through his radio and television. Turn the hotel tv within its cabinet as much as it will rotate, and then position a chair off to the side, your takeout cheesesteak on the bed. From there, you can make out *Wheel of Fortune* on a sliver of the screen. Call home and tell your husband about Tampa. "It's hot," tell him.

"That's what they say about the place."

"Well, they're right. I just hope there's no trouble with the flight Sunday."

"Yeah, well. Me too," he says, then sighs. "So, you figure everything out yet? Everybody clear on what went down in Roswell?"

"Honey, please," you say. "Please don't."

"Isn't that the point? Uncover the government conspiracies and get the bad guys?"

"I don't know," you say, with a forceful breath that surprises yourself. "Maybe it is. Maybe I'll find out tomorrow and maybe I won't. If you want an answer right this second, then I'm afraid you're going to be disappointed. But if you just want to make fun of me, then by all means please continue."

"Ok," Martin says. "Sheesh."

Remind him: "You said you would give me this."

He says, "All right. You're right. I love you."

This conference, Martin said back in Nebraska, is your last chance to do it your way. "What happened happened," he told you. You were at the kitchen table, the late evening light slipping outside the window over the sink. "Samuel's gone," he said. "You need to deal with it. And you're not going to do that by hanging onto these delusions. But go on down to Tampa. Maybe that's the only thing that will convince you. I guarantee you'll see just how crazy these people are."

On the phone now, tell him, "I love you, too." And you do.

Wheel is in the bonus round, but from this angle you can't tell what has been revealed.

• • • •

The next morning, small tables are set on the perimeter of the meeting room. Look around and find each of them half occupied. Approach the nearest one, where a man sits stooped over a coffee. He is a round man in his fifties or perhaps early sixties, with a peninsula of silver hair projecting over the middle of his head. Say, "Excuse me. May I sit here?"

The man glances at you and then back at his coffee on the table, shakes his head. "You people," he says. "You think I'm some kind of fool, don't you? I've seen you outside my house, lady."

"Your house?"

The man snorts something like a laugh and then puts a finger to his temple. "I've got your face right up here. You and your colored friend."

Turn away, your heart double-timing, and find a figure waving to you.

"Tamara, right?" Larry says as you approach.

"Larry," you say.

"This table just opened up, if you're looking for a spot to set your bones."

"Very nice of you."

Sip coffee and tell Larry what the man at the other table said. "That's too bad," Larry says. "Not the way you want to start a day, is it? But I try not to take too much offense. You never know what that man's been put through."

"That's true," you say. You like Larry quite a bit right then. He seems to be a man of immense heart.

Take out your program and discuss what sessions you plan to attend. That evening most everyone will be viewing a film called *Snowden: False Flag or TI Hero?* and then hearing Gloria Downing speak again to wrap up the conference. But until then you can sample from various offerings. Larry says he will be sitting in on "The Electronic Eyes in Your Home," "Fighting Chemtrail Toxins," and "Mind Control from Nazi Germany to Obama's Amerika." Tell him you hope to attend "Everything You Need to Know About Touchless Torture," "Defending Against the Psychiatry Trap," and "Living with Unbelievers." Feel somewhat guilty about that last one, but then picture Martin's eyes rolling and a smirk rising ever so briefly from his usual exhausted frown.

"Do you have someone back home?" you ask.

He eyes you, says, "Might." He fingers a muffin crumb on the table, then breathes and says, "I guess if we can't talk to each other here, we can't talk to anybody anywhere. I got a wife. Got two kids from a different marriage."

"Your wife, does she believe you?"

"She believes . . ." he starts, then pauses. "Tell the truth, I'm not sure what she believes. She's seen what I've seen. Seen those planes in the sky over our house. She can't deny that. She saw what happened to me when I used that microwave she brought home."

"What happened?"

"Strangest thing," Larry says. "I went into something I guess you'd call a trance. Like I was there, but not there. Sort of watching myself."

"And your wife was there."

"She was there. Like I said, she's seen it all, but there's something that won't let her really get it, you know?"

"I do."

"I send her the links. I give her all the information. I photocopy pages out of Gloria's books. Highlight key sections. But then I come home and she's using the dang microwave again. Won't let me get rid of it. I don't understand. And I don't want to think . . ." He shakes his head.

"I'm sure she's not," you tell him.

"No," Larry says. "She's not. She's my lady. If she was, I don't think I could go on, you know?" He tugs at his earlobe, squints off past you. "Now she might be sick. Getting a bunch of tests done. Supposed to get the results today. I don't know how much to trust a doctor, but what are we supposed to do? In fact . . ." He shifts in his seat and looks down toward his lap.

"You know," you whisper, "we're not supposed to have our phones in here."

"I know," Larry says. "But if she gets the results."

"I won't tell," you say.

A man passes by in wraparound sunglasses, a Marines cap, and a t-shirt that reads *Gun Control Isn't about Guns. It's about Control.*

Say to Larry, "My husband isn't a believer."

"Tell you to relax? You're reading too much into things?"

"You've heard it, then?"

Larry smiles. "Yeah, once or twice. That was my ex-wife to a T. 'You're being paranoid.' All right, keep those eyes closed, Charlene."

"Martin's been trying to get me to see a psychiatrist."

Larry exhales loudly and shakes his head. "That old song. Boy, people want the government up in their heads so bad they're willing to pay for it."

"Thing is, though, he's going to leave me. If I don't go, I mean. If I don't try a psychiatrist, probably get on medication, then he's going to leave."

"He told you that?"

Nod. The words not coming.

Larry sips his coffee. "Man," he says. "That's a tough one. I'm sorry to hear that." Larry's kindness sets off a small sadness in you. He reminds you that there are good people in the world. But that reminder is accompanied by the fact that these are the very same people who get attacked, cheated, and targeted by the other ones. Perhaps because of their goodness. It makes them vulnerable.

Ask Larry, "Do you ever think it would just be easier if we did just go to the doctors like everyone wants us to? And let them give us the pills?"

"Tamara," Larry says, "I *know* it would be easier."

"But it wouldn't be living, would it?"

"No, ma'am, it wouldn't."

"Thinking you're free isn't the same as being free." As you say the words, realize that you feel more alive, more in control of your own destiny, than you have in years.

• • • •

Later, Larry sits, to your surprise and delight, with John, the leader of the psychiatry discussion group that just adjourned.

"You've met Tamara, then," Larry says to John.

"I have, I have," John says, as the two men stand and gesture toward a third chair. "If we have time," he says, "I'd like to talk further about your predicament with your husband." In the group, you mentioned Martin's desire for you to seek treatment.

"I would like that."

He says, "You never know who's had access to him. I'm not saying your husband is an agent. I'm sure he thinks he has your best interests at heart. But these are clever, slippery outfits. People work on their behalf for years, their whole lives, without ever even knowing it."

"That's the absolute truth," Larry says.

"I wonder," John says, setting a finger to his lips. "I wonder if I could get you a couple minutes with Gloria. No one knows how to navigate this stuff like her."

Stay calm. Try not to show the excitement alight in you. Say, "That would be wonderful." A private meeting with Gloria Downing is more than you could have hoped for. She is the reason you're there, the one who, though her books and videos, helped you to start understanding what is happening.

"I'll see what I can do. But for now, I want you two to hear me on this. You can survive everything they throw at you. You can. You're here, and that's the first step. Just being open to the truth."

John excuses himself, and Larry raises his eyebrows at you. "A private meeting with Gloria Downing?" he says.

"I know," you say.

"This is your day, girl."

· · · ·

You do not have too much interest in chemtrails but join the discussion group anyway because Larry is going to it and you feel a warm camaraderie with him. You like sitting next to him and think perhaps the feeling is mutual. Nine people sit in a circle of folding chairs. Your comfort is only curtailed by the presence of the man with the silver peninsula of hair, the one who mistook you for whoever has been stationed outside his house.

Next to him, a gaunt, lanky man is speaking. "It took so long to put it together," he says. He is lean like a runner, but unhealthy-looking, with gray skin and broken teeth and eyes sunk back into his face. You've seen that look on too many faces around Omaha over the past decade. "And then I started noticing that the blackouts would happen the day after one of these planes went by with their goddamn trails." He exhales a bitter laugh. "You see little kids and their parents looking up at these things, pointing, thinking how *neat* they are." Larry nods his head. The man goes on, "And then a year or so ago I'm at this party full of government people. Don't ask me how I got in. If I told you, I'd have to kill you." The rest of the circle smiles. "And I'm standing there with a man I realize is a high-up at the Air Force. It's just me and him. And so I say to him, I say, 'You know who I am, don't you?' And he just nods, this fucking fucker. And so I say, 'It's you all who's been knocking me out and stealing my memories, isn't it?' And you know what he says to me? I swear to Christ he looks straight at me and says, 'When'd you find out?'"

A chill scurries up your back. The others in the circle shake their heads and grumble about sons of bitches. Your mind is so focused on the man and his story that you jump when a hand lands softly on your shoulder.

"I'm sorry." It is John, kneeling next to you and whispering close to your ear. "I didn't mean to startle you."

"It's fine," you tell him, your heart still thumping away.

"I'm wondering if you would be interested in that one-on-one with Gloria I mentioned."

. . . .

It is a room nearly identical to yours: the same gray-and-black comforter on the bed, the same thick gray-and-burgundy curtains over the windows, the same tv cabinet. The only difference is this one has Gloria Downing in a rounded club chair in the corner, smoking a cigarette, slipping the filtered end behind her mask to get a drag.

"I shouldn't, I know," Gloria says as John leads you further into the room. "On top of my health, they're probably going to charge me to steam the smell out of the curtains. Do you mind?"

To other people you might say yes, but this is Gloria Downing. "Not at all."

Gloria watches you for a moment, then stubs out the cigarette. "Of course you do," she says. "And you're correct to. Why should I have the right to inflict this on you? Please sit."

There is no other chair, so you sit on the bed and wish you had something stiffer and less intimate under you. The soft mattress feels inappropriate.

Try not to stare. But how strange it is to be in Gloria's presence, up close, to see the eyes you have watched so many times on YouTube, to notice now the crow's feet developing around them, the corona of hazel flecks around her blue eyes. Gloria is probably not much older than you, mid-forties perhaps.

"John tells me you're being pressured into psychiatry," Gloria says. Notice something in her voice you've never registered before, a slight slurring of the "S" sounds.

"My husband would like for me to start seeing someone, yes," you tell her.

"He's worried about you."

Nod your head weakly and feel a sudden surge of longing for Martin and for the world before everything started. Avert your eyes, but know that it is no use. You can feel Gloria watching you imagine the world without Martin. It would be no world at all.

"Tell me about Samuel."

Your son's name shoots through the air and stabs you in the chest. "How do you know about him?"

"It wasn't hard to find out. Tell me what happened."

Choke back the sob rising in your chest. You need to say this. Tell her, "They gave me something. The doctors and nurses. They gave me something so I couldn't produce milk." You've never told anyone but Martin about what happened. Speak as clearly as you can, but don't try to hide it when your hands begin to shake. "They told me I had an infection but couldn't say exactly what kind. Sammy and I were there for a week. Different people would come into the room, men, in the night, and they'd give me things, inject things into my IV. When I'd ask what it was, they wouldn't say anything, and when I asked the doctors the next morning, they would tell me no one had given me anything."

"How did they explain what you saw?"

"They said I dreamed it. Or imagined it. Like you'd say to a little kid. When I insisted, they started in about my mental state. Asking me about my parents and grandparents, all that." Wipe your nose with the sleeve of your shirt. Accept a small box of tissues from John, who has remained by the door. "And so we started giving the baby formula, but they were putting something into that too."

"To make him sick," Gloria says.

"He lived until he was just over a year. They were watching us the whole time. Like they did what they did to Sammy and then wanted to see how we reacted to it. You talk about this in your book."

"Doubling," Gloria says. "Medical experiments become psychological experiments become social experiments. It's economical for them to retain the same subjects."

"That's it. And it just keeps going. I lost my job. Martin is going to leave me. I guess they got a good one."

Gloria looks at John, then back to you. "You should do it," she says. "You should go see a shrink. Let him ask you questions about your childhood and give you medicine to help you cope with what happened."

Watch her eyes, try to understand. Psychiatry is the enemy of truth. It is the medical wing of the whole vicious structure that keeps Gloria and Larry and thousands of other people in states of constant terror. You learned this from Gloria herself. Ask her, "Why are you saying this?"

"Because none of it is real. There is no nefarious organization out there going after people. There is no central headquarters, no government operatives. You haven't been targeted, Tamara. Neither have I, and neither has anyone else."

Shake your head. "You're tricking me."

"I'm not."

"Then why would you do all of this? The videos and the books and this conference?"

"For money," Gloria says quickly. "Don't be naïve." She nods her head toward the door. "All those people out there, they're delusional. They're sick, d'you understand that? They're untethered from reality. And so are you."

Gloria reaches a hand to the side of her head and unhooks the mask hanging from behind her ears. See the absence where her left jaw should be, the crater just below her high cheekbone, the bumpy, shiny skin stretched taut. The tears that have been suppressed only by the strangeness of the situation now fall from your eyes. Gloria leans forward.

68

"Your son died because sometimes children die. It is as simple as that. Just the way I lost my jaw. Bone cancer. It just happens."

"That's not right," you say. And then you feel a new understanding rise out of the fog of sorrow. "It's you," you say. "It's been you all along."

"No," Gloria tells you.

"And now I'm supposed to go out there and tell someone what you've told me and they tell someone else. People start talking on the discussion boards." Don't let your voice crack. Don't give her the satisfaction. "Then we have nothing, and so we might as well listen to everyone telling us we're crazy. You have every angle covered, don't you?" Feel yourself collapsing, slipping away—your body, mind, soul, all of it falling inward like sand into a hole. Fight the urge to reach across and wrap your hands around the woman's throat, to choke the life out of her. You've never felt this way before. It is so simple, so terrifying and beautiful. "Why are you doing this to me?" you ask her. "Why me?"

Gloria's head tilts to the side. "I'm sitting right here telling you that nothing I said last night is the truth, and still you believe that there are people out there after you trying to ruin your life?"

"I know what I know."

Gloria takes a deep breath through her nose and again looks over to John, then back at you.

"Good," she says.

"What do you mean, 'good'?"

"What do you think of the other people out there? There aren't too many women here; I'm sure you noticed."

Thrown by the non sequitur, you simply say, "There's a few."

"A few. Always a few." Gloria stands and sits next to you on the bed. Lean back, away from the woman. Think that this might be the end—finally—that Gloria is going to kill you, stick you with a needle filled with some classified substance, making it look like the sad suicide of a sad woman who'd lost her mind.

Instead, she sets a hand on top of yours.

"Ok, I want to tell you something now," she says. "You aren't crazy. I do believe you. I'm sorry for what I've put you through since you came into this room. John told me about you and I wanted to meet you, but I had to be sure about how deeply you understand what is happening to you. How unshakable your belief is. You are the embodiment of strength, Tamara." Gloria pats your hand, smiles with the intact side of her face. "But there are people out in that room who *are* out of their minds. It's just the truth. They can't tell a bee from a buzz saw. But you. You are legitimate. Now," she says, getting a cigarette from her pack and lighting it. "I'm going to smoke. I apologize. They're not actually that bad for you anyway."

Watch her take a drag.

"Aside from myself, everyone at the front of our movement are men. You know who they are. Screaming, sweating, red-faced men. They get attention, but they make us all look crazy because they act like lunatics. We can't have any more of that. Or at the very least we need other people to counterbalance them. Do you understand what I'm saying?"

"No," you say.

The side of Gloria's mouth curls into a smile. "Sure you do."

Your chest tightens. Your lips tremble. You do understand. "You want me?"

"No," Gloria says. "We need you."

"What does that mean?"

"It means I want you to help lead the movement. I want you to come with us."

"Come with you where?"

"San Diego," Gloria says. "That's where we're based. I've just told you something that only six other people in the world know. This is the trust I have in you. We will help so many people."

"What about my husband?"

"The one who wants you to go to a psychiatrist?"

Look at your hands in your lap. You love Martin but have felt so lost for so long, so absent from your own life. You've felt like a puppet. Here, though, with Gloria, you are a person.

"Can he come with us?"

"No," Gloria says. "I'm sorry, but no."

Grief pulls at you like a hangman's noose. It is that grief that comes just before a person is gone. You can see it happening but have no way to stop it. You know the feeling too well.

"Can I say goodbye?" The words hurt to speak.

"On the phone, not in person. We'll leave from here. Tonight. It isn't ideal, I know, but we've learned from experience that people lose the power they've found once they go back to the site of their torment. You'll be a new person." Gloria puts a hand on your shoulder. "I know you love him," she says. "I can see that. And now, having met you, I know he loves you, too. How could he not? But that's exactly why he will forgive you."

Look at Gloria, her whole beautiful, disfigured face. Ask her, "Why do they do it? Why do they target us?"

And know that your mind is made up even before she says to you, "Let's find out together."

· · · ·

The conference room is too bright for your eyes, the murmuring din of the people inside too droning, like the buzzing of a defective refrigerator. Stop a few steps from the door you exited just thirty minutes before. At the far side of the room, your group remains. Larry's face is pointed to someone across from him, his brow furrowed. It seems like no one has moved. How could that be? Your life has changed since you were last here.

John stands at your side. "Ok?"

"Yes."

"Try to go on like normal," he says.

The floor feels like dough. Steady yourself and focus on your chair. Make your way. The image of Martin flashes hazily in your mind, but it is crowded out by other half-formed thoughts and anxieties. The world swirls and you cannot hang on to any one thing, not even your husband. Walk on.

John steps to the edge of the room as you take your spot once again within the chemtrails group. Look at Larry, who does not return the glance. So lost in your own muddled, excited mind are you that it takes a number of seconds to understand that a dispute is taking place. The man with the silver peninsula of hair is across the circle from Larry, directing his voice forward.

"Get it out," the man says, his voice raised. "I know you got a god-damn gizmo in your pocket. What are you doing with it?"

The whole conference room seems to have quieted, and most people are now looking over.

"It's a phone," Larry says.

"You can't have that in here," the group leader says. "The rules are clear."

"I know," Larry says. "Look, I'm waiting to hear from my wife. She's got—"

"Bullshit," the man across the circle spits. "That ain't no phone. I've seen your black ass outside my house. Seen both of you," he says, now aiming his eyes at you.

"You're mistaken," Larry says. He lifts a hand and tugs on his earlobe, a nervous habit you recognize from earlier.

The man stands from his chair and points at Larry. "What was that?" he shouts. "That was a signal, you son of a bitch. Everybody saw it."

Larry looks side to side. All of the fifty or so people in the room watch him, their faces hardened into heightened attentiveness. You can see worry alight in Larry's eyes.

"Now hang on," Larry says.

"Hang on," the man mocks. "No, I'm not hanging on anymore. You gave yourself away, my brother."

"I'll show you. It's a phone."

And then the man with the silver peninsula of hair pulls from his jacket pocket a small black gun.

Feel a tiny grief sprout deep in your belly.

· · · ·

Your body is still adjusting to the new medications, so Martin takes the wheel the entire seven-hour drive from Omaha to Norman, Oklahoma. Your eyelids fall and your mind wanders away from the car unpredictably while Martin is talking. The radio plays music softly. Martin is worried about the news riling you up, and so insists on classical the whole way. You're fine with that. You don't want to get riled up. The shooting made national media, of course, strange and scandalous as it must have seemed to outsiders, and contact with some of the coverage has been unavoidable. But you've been doing your best to stay away. You were there. There is nothing else you need to know.

In the passenger seat, breathe steadily to hold back the nausea and do your best to ignore the cars following yours, the faces watching from passing windows, the high-pitched whir coming from the vent in front of you. Reach into your shoulder bag and take out the journal Dr. Levi gave you. Note the cars, the faces, the whir. Add them to the growing list of thoughts you will discuss on Thursday.

"Here we go," Martin says as he pulls into the parking lot. Police officers and a handful of reporters stand just off the funeral home grounds, watching.

You spoke to the police, told them everything that had happened in that hotel ballroom in Tampa. The way the man raised the gun and moved it between Larry and you. The way someone in the crowd yelled, "Shoot the motherfuckers!" The way Larry said softly, "Let the lady go, at least."

You endured the officers' glances at one another as the purpose of the conference became clear, and you knew what they were thinking: a gathering of crazies, of paranoids, of people who thought everyone— even each other—was after them. Was it any surprise that blood got spilled? No, it was no surprise.

After Larry's body slumped to the floor, the man with the silver peninsula of hair dropped his gun and ran toward the door, only to be tackled by a group of attendees, who proceeded to beat him wildly. It made no sense. No one knew who was who, and so they simply formed a circus of violence. You watched in horror, somehow standing, some-how stumbling backward through a side door into a hall, where people dashed for stairwells. Along with the shock and grief for the death of this good-hearted man and the guilt of having been, at least by your mere presence, a part of the mess that resulted in his murder, you also felt a profound shame. No surprise at all.

No reporters approached you at the hotel. Probably you blended in with the confused and frightened guests unassociated with the confer-ence. And you never again spoke to Gloria or John or any of the other organizers. Nor did you want to. In that moment when you thought you might die, you longed for nothing but your home and husband— no new life, no lost past, no elusive truth. You knew you would let Mar-tin find a psychiatrist and do as the doctor told you, take the medicine. You would do anything.

Gloria's group, the Coalition of Targeted Individuals, has declared Larry's killer a false flag, a government plant tasked with undermining the credibility of the organization and its claims. "Jesus," Martin said when you told him this. "Whatever it takes to keep the delusion going." Then he looked at you, a half apology in his eyes.

Martin holds the door of the funeral home open for a trio of older ladies, who smile at him and nod and touch his outstretched arm and say, "Thank you."

His name was not Larry. It was Edwin. Edwin McMichaels, and he was fifty-three years old. A small-engine mechanic whose body is barely visible within the casket at the front of the room.

The room is full and hushed with the murmurings of grief. People sit in metal chairs and rise as others shuffle by. Watch as they hug and console each other, these sad, confused folks, all of them wondering how such tragedies happen. Such incomprehensible tragedies. Watch until that shame returns and presses your head down, eyes to the floor. Let Martin take your hand. Feel him kiss your head. Recall only now that Edwin had a sister also named Tamara, that he revealed this to you. Press up against that shame. Look again at the people around you. Wonder who she is, this other Tamara, doing what she can to hold herself together.

INTERLUDE

CHRISTMAS, WEST TEXAS

. . . .

In a diner out on the arid void of West Texas, the waitress sloshed a little something extra into my coffee, then her own, pointed to the window, and said, "This day last year I seen a UFO, right there over that far mesa." I turned on my stool. The place was empty save for a man in a booth, older than myself and slightly more alone (at least I had the attention of the waitress), and out the window past him I was sure for a quick quarter-moment that I caught sight of a brilliant alien flash in the distance—though it could have been something else, something small and close, an impossibly lost fleck of snow glinting off the diner's neon just before winking into nothing.

TWO

THE CALLER

. . . .

All week Max thinks about it. At night he falls asleep constructing the narrative, and at work he spends the lunch hour in his car manufacturing details. When Sunday night rolls around and Nora has been put to bed and Julia is asleep or reading, he brings the radio station's stream up on his computer. He's in the den and the moon illuminates the snow falling ceaselessly outside. He tells himself he's calling on a lark, a private prank, because he's bored, because as he listens there's a lull in the broadcast, awkward silences that the show's host struggles to fill, admirably, with recitations of stories she's heard, with the importance of being in touch, of reaching out, of a voice, and he just wants to give her someone to talk to. And see, he just happens to have this story at the ready.

He calls because somehow it doesn't actually occur to him that he will be put on the air.

But regardless of why, he does call and the producer, Javier, asks what Max figures must be the standard questions: who he's calling about and where was this person last seen and how long ago.

"Stuart." Max's chest heaves out his brother's name. "Near Juárez," he says. "Just over a year." This is the new history he has constructed for his brother: he went across the border with friends for yucks, got separated from the group after a bout of drinking, was snatched up and held for ransom.

Javier says, "And is there anything specific we can know about Stuart so that if he is listening he will know it is you talking?"

Max thinks for a moment and, at a loss, resorts to another bit of truth. "We always called him Ace," he says.

"That should do," Javier says. "Now when you hear Mariana, she'll say your name and you're on. Just keep calm and talk to Mariana. She's a great listener." He says, "Is your radio on?"

"Yeah," Max says, happy to offer an uncomplicated answer.

"Okay, turn it off or else we get feedback. Can you turn it off for me?"

"Yes," Max says. He feels as if he's being talked through the landing of a plane. He presses pause on the streaming bar on the screen and Mariana's voice, which has for the past hour been humming through the room, goes silent. Aside from the laptop screen, the den is dark.

And then Javier says, "Ok, here's Mariana."

He should hang up. Of course, he knows he should hang up. Right then he should pull the phone from his cheek and let his finger graze the red circle on the screen and then go to bed. Or he should go out. He should step into their bedroom and whisper to Julia that he's antsy, no reason, and that he's going out for a bit, not late, and then he should do this, go out and be among the young and youngish people who populate this town, who drink vespers and bitter beer, who eat salted caramel and forever talk about the salted caramel they just ate, who smile in their stocking caps and craft brewery t-shirts, who work in Max's office or some other office or teach schoolchildren to write in cursive or build computers, who take adult learning classes and join gyms and laugh and talk about how *awkward* they are but who really float through social strata like perfect molecules of gas.

He should hang up.

"Hello Max in Boulder, Colorado," Mariana says in a soothing tone. "We don't get too many calls from Boulder."

She pauses. Max says, "Yeah."

She says, "Who are you calling about tonight?"

"My brother, Stuart," Max says.

"Javier tells me Stuart had a nickname."

"We used to call him Ace," Max says.

"Is that what you'd like me to call him tonight?"

"I guess so."

"What would you like to say to Ace?"

"I don't know."

"Take your time. Say whatever comes to your head."

"I guess," Max says, "I miss him. I guess I want to say that I miss him."

Mariana says, "Anything else, Max?" After a second of silence, she adds, "Do you want to tell Ace about anything in your life? Any news he'd be interested in?"

"Oh," Max says. He goes blank.

"It's okay if you don't," Mariana says. "Some callers like to pass on anything happening in the family."

"My family is good."

"You have children?"

"Yes. A daughter."

"Ace's niece."

"Yes," he says. But how strange, how nonsensical it is to think of her this way, this girl who missed his brother's entire existence by a decade.

"Are your parents living?"

"No."

Mariana asks if Max would like to talk about the circumstances of Ace's disappearance, reminding him that he should not disclose anything crucial to any investigation, and he tells her what he's concocted. Outside Juárez. A year ago. Drinking.

Mariana says she wishes this was a new story.

She thanks him for calling, and he hangs up and flexes his fingers. The skin on the backs of his hands is burning because of the dryness of the air and the heat in the house. He presses the radio on again, and Mariana has moved on to another call, a woman speaking in Spanish. Max tries to catch whatever words he might, but whatever she's saying remains lost.

Max shuts down his laptop. He goes upstairs and moves as softly as he can across the creaking floors outside Nora's room. In his and Julia's bedroom he unbuckles his belt and lets his pants slip to the floor. He slides into the cold sheets, and Julia wakes with a snort. She looks at him, but with eyes that are not yet seeing.

"Sorry," Max whispers. "I was trying not to wake you."

Her body unfolds back onto the bed. "It's good," she just barely verbalizes. "I was having a fucking awful dream about Nora." Her eyes close, and she is again breathing the even breaths of sleep. He listens to her awhile and watches the dark and feels almost as if he's really just spoken to his brother.

. . . .

He found the show a month ago. There was a bit about it on some early Sunday morning NPR program, and he searched for it online right then and listened to the broadcast that night as caller after caller gave the first name of a son, a husband, a boyfriend, almost always a man, who'd disappeared amidst the cartel wars. Most spoke in Spanish. Since Max speaks no Spanish aside from one through ten and the usual greetings and foods, he heard little other than an impenetrable wall of syllables. But then a few called in English, though always with accents of the recently immigrated. They told Mariana the worst things Max had ever heard. Not because they held the gory details of cartel beheadings, of rapes and murders, of the sociopathic criminal under-world's takeover of the cultures of the border towns, but because they had none of that. They weren't even stories these people told. They just talked. They talked, most of them, directly to their missing person, reciting the mundanities of everyday life. Mom's hip is acting up again. Little sister isn't getting much playing time on her soccer team. Dad's been working some overtime at the plant. Max couldn't believe these people. So matter of fact. So dull. He wondered what he would want his people to say if he'd been snatched up and maybe tortured, maybe killed. Something more than what was for dinner last night. Something more than a weekend trip to the grandparents'. He'd want some tears. Goddamn right. He'd want a bit of wailing. Cries of *Why why why*. Some words urged out through clenched teeth. He'd want the good stuff. Terrible, soul-stomping grief.

But there was something he couldn't understand right then. He started listening weekly and heard the same voices again and again and again. The same people each Sunday night passing on the newest news. And he figured, fuck, they've been at this for a while. Calling and calling and hoping to get their person back. And he remembered how grief morphs. How it cannot remain what it is in the early days of loss, when your mind is gone, when the body recoils from the slightest yip of joy, when food cools and coagulates on kitchen tables and days pass and the silence of endless nights falls like a suffocating shroud. How it lessens, lightens. Such is the unsustainability of grief. Eventually, for most, even the most miserable and consuming of heartaches retreat into the crowd of other emotions, other occupations. If it didn't, we wouldn't be here—the vast, inconsolable race of humans would have offed themselves long ago.

· · · ·

Max's cell phone rings a few days later. He is at his office, a wide and warmly decorated expanse of cubicles. The company took care to avoid the fluorescent lights and white walls of traditional offices. Here the walls are a cozy light gray. One has had its brick exposed. The products they make and sell—outdoorsy outerwear of technologically inventive fabrics—are expensive and manufactured in many of the world's least torturous sweatshops. Max works in marketing, specializing in print and billboard advertising. It is a good place to work.

He doesn't recognize the number illuminated on his buzzing phone.

"Hello, Max?" the voice, vaguely familiar, says.

"Yes?"

"This is Javier Florio. From *Voices for the Lost*."

Max wonders for a moment if this is some sort of trick. He can hear his coworkers bouncing ideas off one another on the other side of the half wall. They're debating the audience potential of two women's magazines.

"Are you there, sir?"

"Yes."

"You are Max who called the show?"

His head goes cold. His eyes are drawn to a small rubber ball that has rolled into the back corner of his desk, a stress reliever given out by his bosses at the last team retreat. Dust sticks to the tacky plastic. "Yes, it's me," he says, trying to sound casual for both Javier and whoever might be nearby. "What can I do for you?"

"We try not to reach out to our callers. But, well, it happens every once in a while when we hear something that might help their situation."

"Help?" he says curtly, a subtle rudeness seeming to be his only defense.

"There is a family who called us, not to be on the air but because they heard you this week. They would very much like to speak with you. They're missing someone also, and it seems they feel there might be some connection to your brother. I'm afraid they wouldn't give me many details, so I can't tell you much beyond this. Only that they would like to speak to you. And in my opinion they seemed truthful, for what that is worth. I of course have only my instincts about the situation."

"It seems unlikely that . . ." Max's mind stumbles for words. "That there is a connection."

"The odds are long, yes," Javier says. "People get desperate. I'm not calling to advocate for them. I don't know them. Only to pass on the message and to ask if it is your wish that I give them your number."

"How about you give me their number?" Max says.

"I asked. They said they don't have one. It seemed like maybe money is not good."

"Well, I just . . ." Max lets his words trail. He has nothing.

After a moment, Javier says, "Where did your brother disappear?" His voice has changed. There's a sternness in it, and Max knows he is stuck. Javier's instincts are kicking in.

"Near Juárez," he says.

"Juárez," Javier repeats. "Many stories about abductions in Juárez. This is an unusual place for American boys to go. Not dangerous like it used to be, but still not the best. Why did they go to Juárez?"

"They weren't *in* Juárez. They were just nearby. Sort of adjacent." Max sighs, a performance of exasperation. "Ok, no, it's fine. Give them my number. Go ahead, it's fine."

But he knows it is anything but fine.

• • • •

He waits. Two days. Three days. He works and comes home to his family. He cooks dinner most nights and feels a great sense of satisfaction in the simple and crucial act of laying plates of food before Julia and their child. He and Julia switch off nights reading to her and putting her to bed. He finds that, in aging, he has come to rely on the routine of his

89

life. Where in his younger days he railed against conventions and rules, he now seeks them out. He would like more. More consistency. More predictability. He enjoys what customs they've developed. Dinner. Bath time. The three books before bed, the two songs.

These nights, though, he is distracted, his thoughts fluttering to what he might do if these people call. His mind floats away in the middle of a *Curious George* book, and Nora calls him back. "Daddy, keep *reading*."

That night Julia says, "What's with you?"

The call comes the next morning. He is at work. He lets it go to voicemail, but no message is left. That afternoon, another. Same number. This time there is a message, the voice of a boy who sounds as if he is reading a script.

Hello, Mister Max. My name is Mateo Herrera. I am calling about your brother, Ace. My family would like to talk with you. We have someone also who is gone to the cartels. Also from Juárez at the same time. My cousin Andrés Herrera. Please call us. Thank you, sir.

The boy leaves two different numbers, neither the one that appeared on Max's iPhone. His thumb aims down at the delete button, but he stops short and clicks save instead. He stands in his cubicle and watches a line of four men being led into the glass-walled conference room. On the other side of the office two men from Development stand at the kitchen talking and waiting on espressos. Max cannot remember what he'd been working on prior to the phone call.

・　・　・　・

That night, after dinner and bath and books and songs, after kissing Julia goodnight, after she asks, "You going to be up late?" and he answers, "No, no, just a little while," he goes to the den and opens his laptop and googles "Andrés Herrera." Over 13,000 results appear, most notably for a dentist in California, a film actor—also California—and a soccer player in England. He refines his search: "Andrés Herrera disappearance." For this he gets fewer results, though most of them seem to be just as unconnected. But near the top of the screen is a link for a Facebook group. He clicks and finds the page written in Spanish. The picture is of a man, perhaps nineteen or twenty, handsome, smiling and squinting in the sun with a blue glimmer of ocean behind his shoulder. Under "About," Max finds more Spanish, but below that a translation:

Andrés Herrera disappeared from Juárez, Mexico, on August 12. Nothing has been heard from him since then. No one has seen him. If you have seen Andrés or know where Andrés is please send a message to Mateo Herrera. This page is for people who loved Andrés. Please leave messages for him here. And it is for anyone who wants to give money to his family so they can look for him. God bless you.

Max clicks back to the main page and finds that nineteen people have liked this group. There are no messages for Andrés.

• • • •

Max's brother Stuart started dealing pretty early—as far as the rest of the family and the police could put together, his freshman year. Pot, of course. Some pills, but mostly mild painkillers, nothing too addictive or deadly. He got arrested for possession when he was fifteen. A couple grams. A bowl of residue. Their father paid the piddly fine and made Stuart work it off with chores—doing the lawn, cleaning out the basement—which Stuart completed uncomplainingly. He knew the game. He knew how to back off and give himself over to the system, whether that system was the law or school or mom and dad. "Give 'em what they want," he once said to Max during this punishment phase. But soon, of course, he was back at it.

He started slinging coke sometime in his junior year. Everyone had heard about his run-ins with the police by this point, and while half the school seemed to regard him as a loser and a burnout, the other half, even many of those who would never touch drugs, treated him with a sort of careful reverence. Stuart seemed to hover ever so slightly above the petty high school fray. Max himself was a freshman then and would later recall that period with heavyhearted nostalgia, moments when, walking down the hall between some classroom and another, his brother would come out of nowhere to swing an arm over Max's shoulder and make some comment about whatever girls he got it in his mind that Max should "go for." He would deliver Max to his next class with a slight shove through the door and say something like, "Get 'em, killer." It was never completely clear who he might be referring to—who the 'em was—but it also never seemed to matter much.

Stuart was missing for two days before his body was discovered in the basement of an unfinished house in a half-built new subdivision the next town over. A construction crew found him. He'd been beaten severely and then shot in the head. He was seventeen, a senior. In the weeks and months after Stuart's murder, the family would be questioned (by the police, each other, themselves) about Stuart's behavior just prior to that day. Did he seem different? Did he say anything that caused concern? Was he agitated or on edge?

"He was a teenager," Max's father would say.

"Did you know he was dealing drugs?" the police asked.

"He was selling some pot, but he stopped a while ago," their father said.

"He didn't stop, and I'm afraid it was a bit more than just pot."

The theory that arose was that he'd been killed by other dealers, serious men without much compunction about putting a bullet into some punk-ass kid from the suburbs. The cops questioned people. They held news conferences. But they never made an arrest. Months went by and then years. Their father passed. Sandy, the youngest, just ten when Stuart was killed, got married, and soon had her son. Their mother passed. Max moved away from Chicago, settled in Boulder, rented an apartment just a mile (he found out after signing the lease) from where JonBenét Ramsey was killed. He got married, had Nora, and continued on, waking each morning with a sad amazement at still being alive.

• • • •

Max sees the first post on his Facebook feed. It is Saturday, and he's in Denver with Julia and Nora at the Children's Museum. Kids are crawling through an outsize hamster maze the museum has erected. A boy pulls Nora's foot back, making her pancake onto her belly. "Hey now," Max says. But the kids laugh like mad. Max and Julia are standing off to the side, trying to stay out of the way of foot traffic while still keeping eyes on their girl. Julia says, "I'm so tired today."

Max purses his mouth in a way that is meant to communicate sympathy, but he feels quite good. Relaxed and energized. Nearly two weeks have passed since the Herreras have last called (they stopped leaving messages after three, stopped trying his number at all after five). This was the first morning in that time that Max did not wake with the sensation of being watched, the first without a vague weight of shame resting atop his chest.

In a moment of benign parental neglect, he pulls his phone from his pocket and presses the "F" icon on the screen. Many pictures of children. Links to *Times* articles. GIFs of mismatched animals cuddling. Then it appears: a picture of some rundown Mexican border city and the words "Who Is Ace? The Mystery of a Missing Colorado Man." Max stares at the words as if confronted by some bit of nonsense from a dream. His hand beginning to tremble, he taps the link. Stacked along the right-hand side of the page are thumbnails and headlines about fracking and Citizens United and the legacy of Occupy. But the bulk of the screen is taken by a short entry:

> Two weeks ago a Boulder man called a radio show that attempts to communicate with people kidnapped by drug cartels. While the vast majority of callers reside near the U.S.-Mexico border, the call from Boulder has piqued interest. Identified only as "Max," the man tells the story of his brother Stuart (nicknamed "Ace"), who went across the border with friends and was abducted while out drinking. "Max" did not say whether or not the kidnappers have reached out with ransom or demands. This story begs a few important questions: One, what are the police doing (or not doing) to find the missing man? And two, why have we not heard about this case? As politicians on both sides of the aisle try to curry favor with constituents on the immigration issue by celebrating their own successes and exaggerating their opponents' failures, one must ask, what stories are not making it to the so-called nightly news? Most importantly, where is Ace, and how many Aces are out there? (Link to *Voices for the Lost* below.)

Max feels as if his sense of the reality of his life is slipping away from him like a snake into a hole. He is dizzy and puts a hand out to steady himself against the wall of the museum.

Nora dashes off to the water-play room, and Julia follows quickly. Max moves as if pushing against a great and unrelenting wave. Julia is saying something about a kid at Nora's pre-K who's been giving her a hard time.

"She's mentioned him twice now," she says. "It's like, at what point do you say something to the teacher? How do we know when things move into bullying?"

"Bullying?" Max says, the word momentarily bringing him back to the world.

His phone, still in hand, buzzes.

"Hello, Max. This is Javier from *Voices for the Lost*. I'm sorry to bother you on a Saturday, but we've gotten a few more calls about you and your brother."

"Yes," Max says, unsurprised. "I'm trying to figure out . . ." What is he trying to figure out?

"Who is that?" Julia mouths, brow furrowed. She's slipping a plastic poncho over Nora's head. It's backward, though, and before Julia rights the garment Nora pulls the transparent hood onto her face and sucks the plastic into her open mouth.

"For whatever reason," Javier says, "the situation seems to be of interest to people."

"I guess so," Max says.

"This is a good thing, Max. Of course our primary goal at the show is to provide a line of communication between those lost and those looking. But it has happened in the past that their stories have caught on with the public. This is rare, and normally it is with the public on the other side of the border. My question for you is whether you want me to give out your number. I'm afraid I don't have the time to relay messages between you and anyone who gets in touch with the show; I'm sure you understand. I suppose what I need from you is a blanket yes or no."

"Right, right," Max says. "Absolutely, I wouldn't want to put you in the position . . ."

Julia watches him quizzically as Nora splashes in shallow basins, sends a tiny boat down a lazy river.

Javier says, "It's not so easy. You probably would like to tell the story and see what you can get moving. But there's a danger, too."

"Danger?"

Julia puts her fists on her hips and tilts her head. She mouths *What is it*?

95

"I don't know what has transpired between your family and those holding Ace, but it could be they might be interested in you, or another member of your family. These are brazen and ruthless people. You cannot underestimate them. Many of them are children themselves. Teenagers. They do not understand what a life is or what it means to take one. I've been producing the show for six years now. The stories I've heard are hard to forget. You do not want to be any more involved with them than you are. I don't say this to scare you but to help you understand the situation."

Is Max putting his family in danger? Could this charade somehow become real? Jesus, he feels sick. Javier is saying something about the police in Mexico, but Max can't follow. He thinks he might faint. Or vomit into the water-play basins. Julia is now standing right in front of him, staring up at him. Nora—twenty, twenty-five feet away—disappears behind the hips of a heavyset woman for an interminable two seconds, then reappears on the other side.

"No," Max says into the phone, interrupting Javier. "Don't give my number out. Don't tell anyone anything about me."

．．．．

Julia sits at the dining room table. She says, after a full minute of silence, "It's just a weird thing to do."

"I know."

"I saw the link on Facebook from a couple people. I didn't click on it, though. The audio of the call is there?"

"Yeah."

"You know someone is going to listen and recognize your voice."

"I'm hoping not, but yeah, maybe."

Julia hasn't looked at him, instead training her eyes on the painting on the opposite wall, one of her own from college. "Have you thought that you couldn't talk to me about your brother? I'm not trying to make this about me, but I want to know if you've felt like you didn't want to talk to me about it."

"No, no," Max says.

"You can talk to me."

"I know that. It was an impulse."

"Do you think you should see a therapist or something?"

"Jesus, no," he says. "No, I just want to get on with things. It was a weird thing to do but I did it and now it's on the fucking internet."

Julia says, "You should probably stay away from Facebook and all that for a while, in case it doesn't go away."

And here again is that old shame pressing down.

• • • •

It doesn't go away. At breakfast a couple days later, Julia says, "I think you probably need to look."

Max continues to cut Nora's waffle. He breathes, says, "I don't want to."

"What don't you want to do?" Nora asks.

"Be awake," Max says.

Nora puts her head down on the table and pretends to sleep. "I'm not awake, Daddy," she says.

She lays down her head and mimics snoring in a cartoonish *ka-shooo, ka-shooo*. A piece of waffle falls from her mouth.

Julia says, "Sweetie, you're getting syrup in your hair."

"Two more days," Max says. "I'll give it two more days and see what happens."

"It's kind of blowing up," Julia says. Max says nothing. "People are getting pissed."

"Language," Nora says.

"Pissed?" Max says.

"*Language*," Nora says.

"What are people getting upset about?"

Julia says, "Well, the initial thing was *Where is he*? But now there's something else. Will you just look at it? There's a thing on HuffPo."

After the school bus picks Nora up, Max finds the article. It doesn't so much dwell on Stuart—or, rather, the fictitious "Ace"—as it uses Max's call as a jumping-off point. In the time Max was unplugged the story reached as far as the MSNBC website (Max's eyes going blurry with anxiety at this revelation), with various writers calling for a more rigorous investigation into not only this disappearance but the disappearances of any and all U. S. citizens abducted for ransom or collateral in the cartel wars. This, according to the *Huffington Post* article, is all well and good, but it goes on to call the media out on its bias, positing (correctly, Max has to admit, even in the midst of what he can only understand as an out-of-body experience) that it is only the assumed whiteness of "Ace" that has evoked the concern of the internet's legions.

Do we feel our hearts drop at the news of yet another brown-skinned person gunned down or disappeared in these new quasi-militia states? Do we voice our outrage? Write insistent emails to our leaders? Do we even *care*? Or do we instead simply ride a wave of apathy, inured to the violent deaths of nonwhites, comfortably resigned to the *way it is*?

It is a good article—well written and without dull platitudes, easy answers, or pandering claims—the kind of article Max himself might post on his own Facebook page, along with some particularly impactful quote, were it not for the fact that it is about him. He tells himself not to read the comments, but of course he does anyway. These are less considered than the article itself. How angry people are, and how they seem to cherish their anger above all else. He bemoans the exaggerated outrage of the anonymous internet commenter but knows that in this case he cannot lay blame entirely at the feet of the web's rageful tendencies.

In this case, Max is to blame.

He thinks of Andrés Herrera and the nineteen people praying for his return and how Andrés Herrera is probably dead.

That morning Max tries to work on a new billboard campaign aimed at the Southwest, but it is no use. His mind can't stay on anything for more than a few seconds at a time. At 11 o'clock he texts his boss *Not feeling great. Heading home but I'll be available,* and his boss texts back *Feel better bro.*

His phone rings as he pulls through an icy lake of slush and into the driveway of his house. It is a number he does not recognize, but just then he is feeling too low to resist.

"Hello?"

"Is this Max Shelenberg?"

"Yes."

"My name is Charlotte Givens. I write for the *Denver Post.* Are you the brother of the late Stuart Shelenberg?"

He exhales, suddenly exhausted. "Yes."

"Did you call a radio show called *Voices for the Lost* on the night of February 19?"

He unhooks his seatbelt and leans up to peer over the hood of his Forester. An army of icicles hangs from his gutters, dripping in the sun. The melt-off is pooling at the door of the garage. He will have to salt before evening falls.

"Yes," he says.

"Do you mind answering a few questions?" Charlotte Givens asks.

"Sure," Max says.

Fuck it already.

. . . .

Highlights from the *Post* article include . . .

Mr. Shelenberg referred to the call as a "severe lapse in judgment," adding that he "just wasn't thinking straight."

And . . .

Producer Javier Florio says that they have no plans to alter their vetting process for callers. "We don't know of any other instances like this in our ten years of broadcasting the show," Mr. Florio said. "We are a small program built on a foundation of trust. People call us because they trust that we will not judge them or their loved ones who have been taken in the terrible wars among the cartels. And we must return that trust." Asked if he thought the situation with Mr. Shelenberg would result in more bogus calls, he said, "I don't know. I hope not."

And . . .

But this is not to say that everything in the story was completely fabricated. Mr. Shelenberg did in fact have a brother named Stuart, nicknamed Ace, who was murdered in suburban Chicago in 1998. According to police in the town of Schaumburg, Illinois, the case remains open and no arrests have ever been made.

. . . .

"Did we call him that?" Max's sister asks. She sits down on the sofa, takes off her shoes and lets out a groan of relief. Sandy flew out from

O'Hare that morning to be with Max, to help him out through the ordeal of the story breaking. On the phone two days before, he'd told her no, no, god, don't bother yourself with this, but she insisted. She said she wanted to be there for him. "Family," she'd said, as if the word summed up with perfect clarity the reasons we do anything.

"I guess I kind of remember," she goes on. "But it was more like a jokey thing, wasn't it?"

"I don't think it was totally jokey," Max says.

"Or just a Dad thing?"

"No," Max says. "It was everybody. Everybody called him Ace."

In actuality, now that Max thinks about it, they rarely called Stuart "Ace." And it *was* mostly their father. Somewhere along the way, though, this name, common or not, has taken on significance for Max. He likes to think of his brother this way. He likes to think of Stuart as being worthy of such a name. As if the world saw him, took careful note, and bestowed it upon him.

Sandy goes to the window. "I guess I just don't remember. Maybe I was just younger," she says, though she is just a few years Max's junior. She is done with the topic. She tosses the curtains of the window open, and a blinding blanket of light overtakes the room. "Jesus Christ, you people get a lot of snow here."

Julia comes home with Nora and Max volunteers to cook steaks on the grill.

"It's freezing out, Max," Julia says.

"Colder in Chicago, really," Sandy says. "But yeah, it's a stupid idea."

"Well, that's my thing," Max says. "Stupid ideas."

"Max," Julia says.

"No, come on, it'll be good. Hell with the cold. We'll have steaks. I'll be in and out. I'll bundle up."

In the weeks since the *Post* article, he's felt himself fluctuating between manic peaks and depressive trenches. This is a peak. Everything will blow over. Everything will be *fine*. It is all so goddamn laughable. What was he so worried about the day before, when he could barely inch out of bed to make breakfast, when he spent his lunch break in his car, eyes closed, trying intensely to think of nothing? Everything will be fine.

But regardless of his ups and downs, the talk continues—the blog posts, the comments, the discussions on local NPR, even a short mention on a Rocky Mountain PBS program devoted to issues concerning the state's Hispanic population.

The general condemnation: Max is a white man, with all the privileges this allows him, appropriating another culture's pain to prop up his own sense of victimhood.

The general defense: Ok, yeah, probably, but he did lose a brother for real, so maybe that lets him off the hook a wee bit?

Sandy, now on the third day of her visit, stands in the doorway of the den. "Dude," she says. "It's still snowballing. They were talking about you on *The Fan*."

"The what?"

"Maybe it's called something else."

"The fucking sports station?"

"Yeah," she says. "Part of the Broncos recap."

"Why?"

"I guess one of the players mentioned you in a postgame. I don't know his name. I tuned in right in the middle. But isn't that crazy? Guy's there in his towel, just won a game, and *you're* what's on his mind." She comes in and sits. "One of my friends linked to something a guy in Singapore wrote. *Singapore*."

Max says, "I'm not trying to be a dick, but aren't you needed at home?"

Sandy says, "I'm dealing with a family emergency."

· · · ·

Max remembers the weeks that followed Stuart's murder like some terrible experimental film. Great expanses of silence descending upon the world. Their parents floating through the house uttering nothing. Sandy in the backyard, playing with friends whose parents stood stiffly against the side fence. Normally they'd have just dropped their girls off and come back later. Or if they had stayed, Max's mom or dad would have invited them in for coffee or an iced tea. But now they just remained there on the periphery of the yard.

The silence was broken only by growls about the cops and the investigation. They said, "Well, why don't they just . . ." and "Haven't they even . . ." and "They need to tell us *more* . . ." The problem—it was so obvious to Max's parents—was that the cops were strangers. People doing a job. Why should they care about finding the men who killed their son? The police followed protocols and filled out forms, but protocols and forms did not track the killers of boys. First shift, second shift, third shift—pointless. All these men and women clocking in and covering their beats accomplished nothing. There was only one thing that meant anything in the world, only one energy that the parents of a slain teenager could own, and that was anger.

So they became angry.

Confusion, grief, and just plain old sadness all transmuted into a great gray ire. It escaped them like puffs of breath in the cold. It was there while they ate dinner in silence. It was there in the mornings, getting Max and Sandy out the door to school. It was there when his mother quit her job. It was in their clenched jaws when they met Max in the guidance counselor's office after he carved *Fuck this shit* into a locker door with a Swiss Army knife. Did words even pass the lips of those in that room? Not to his recollection. Just blank, stony eyes. Did the television have volume for those months? Was there music in the world? Did even the sobs and screams that contorted their faces emit the slightest of chirps to break the relentless muting of their lives?

And then one morning, ten months after, Max's mother said, "Let's go to the beach." It was early March and the world was still frozen solid. "The Dunes. We haven't been there in years. Sandy, you probably don't even remember the last time, you were so small."

"I wasn't that small," Sandy said.

"Well," their mom said. "Still."

On the way they stopped at Dunkin' Donuts and got a dozen doughnuts and coffees for the parents up front and hot chocolates for Max and Sandy in back. Max drank coffee when he was with his friends, crowding into booths at Denny's and smoking cigarettes and accepting refill after refill from one poor waitress or another, but he still had a sweet tooth and happily took the chocolate. By the time they crossed over into Indiana his body vibrated. It was a sort of euphoria, brought on not just by the sugar buzzing through his veins, but by being away from home and school, from streets whose pavement might as well have been poured and spread by Stuart himself, for all their inseparableness.

What Max remembers most clearly is the stinging of the glacial wind on his cheeks. He pulled his knit hat down further to cover his earlobes. His nose froze, inside and out. Sandy marched out ahead of the rest, as if she had a destination amidst this barren beach, an appointment to keep. Their mom was next, her shoulders high and her hands shoved deep in the pockets of her camel hair overcoat. Max went forward, taking occasional glances back at his father, bringing up the rear. They were four now, just four. A terrible number. Incomplete.

His dad came up beside him, said, "This is good, being out here."

"It's awful," Max said. The sugar crash coming.

His dad swung an arm around Max's shoulder, pulled his hat back, and kissed his forehead. Max pulled his hat down again. "You know what it's like when I touch you?" his dad said. "You can't know. I never knew. It's like I'm touching the future and the past all at once."

"O-*K*," Max said, an irresistible edge of teenage shittiness in his voice.

His dad said, "It's like touching god."

"So I'm god?" Max said.

His dad nodded. "Something like that."

"Is Sandy god, too?"

"Yes."

A blast of wind took Max's breath away. When he could breathe again he said, "Was Stuart god?"

"Yeah," his dad said after a moment. "He was god."

Sandy and their mom were at the water, and for a good long while the four of them stood mesmerized by the steadiness of the white-peaked waves. And for a moment Max understood why everything came out of his parents as anger. How else to feel when someone murders your god?

. . . .

Max gives a couple of interviews over the phone for *Slate* and *Salon*. He apologizes. Says it was a stupid thing to do. He feels bad for lying and for wasting people's energy. Says he wants to move on but that he understands it isn't up to him. He started this thing and he will have to see it through until it is over. Thankfully, they only briefly ask about the real Stuart. Max doesn't want to get into that. He is doing this to apologize, and he knows that any hint of making it about his tragedy will put him back at the beginning. He wants it to be over.

Sandy sticks around for a few more days. The night before she leaves she stands in the living room and speaks to her husband on the phone. "Don't let the house be a wreck when I get in," she tells him. "Defy the cliché, man."

Max will miss her. They stay up late that night talking and promising each other they'll get the kids together soon.

A month goes by. Max is again able to work undistractedly. Nora able to stop asking about their parents' whispered conversations. That old shame weighing down on Max's chest eases up just a bit.

And then *Storyline* happens.

Max has heard of it. Everyone has. A long-form true crime podcast that emerged out of the popularity of others like *Serial*. A copycat, most said at first, but one that quickly eclipsed the others in listenership. The last series they did investigated the collapse of a coal mine in eastern Kentucky. Before that they probed a rape charge in the upper ranks of the Navy.

Now they wanted to solve a murder.

The email comes from the producer. After a brief history of the program—the results and impact of the first few series—she writes, "Your brother's case came to our attention through the situation with *Voices of the Lost*, and while we cannot say where the case will take us, I can assure you that this is not our primary concern and will not be at the core of our investigation as we envision it. In our preliminary research we've found a number of distressing abnormalities in police procedure. These may prove to be of no consequence, and many or all might be cleared up in the course of the investigation. But the fact remains that your brother was murdered and no one has been held responsible. This is what drives us."

It has been so long since Max allowed himself to dream about his brother's murder being solved. Years since his last fantasy of facing the killer in a courtroom, of hearing the word *guilty*, of finding a vessel for his own anger. The attention he would have to endure means nothing.

He emails the producer: "Anything you need."

· · · ·

The producers are a team, two women and a man, based in Manhattan. They make Max feel old and frumpy and provincial, but he does his best to ignore this. They come to Boulder, set up a mic and laptop, and he talks. They fly him into O'Hare and he stays with Sandy and the two of them are mic'd and they stroll their old neighborhood and they talk. They bring him to New York and he is faced with boxes upon boxes of files and photographs that the producers have amassed and he sleeps in a good hotel near their offices in Midtown. He talks more than he has talked in years. Or so it feels. They prompt him with questions about things he has never thought to connect with Stuart's killing: gym class, names he hasn't heard in years, the smoking section at Denny's. He does not ask where their questions are heading. In his off time he walks through a frigid Chinatown and listens to the voices of the world swirl around him and visits the World Trade Center Memorial and Face-times with Julia and Nora—but mostly he sits in the studio and he talks.

· · · ·

By the time the first episode of *Storyline* is posted, more than a year has passed since he called *Voices for the Lost*. Max hears his own voice and Sandy's voice and the voices of police and FBI and Chicago news personalities. He hears Stuart's old schoolmates, his old drug custom-ers. He hears strangers hypothesizing about what happened to Stuart. And only then does he truly understand that this story is once again *out there*, that he has been thrust back into the pain and chatter. Back when it happened there were the local news and the papers and the radio. That was bad, but now there is the internet.

Max quits Facebook and Twitter. With the exception of work and the show itself, he stays offline entirely. Each Sunday night after Nora has gone to bed, he and Julia sit in the den and listen to the story of his brother's death unfold. When it is over they close the laptop. They say nothing about it. In silence, they take themselves to bed, and in the warmth of the covers Julia turns to her husband and pulls his face to her neck, inviting him to her.

• • • •

The producers have a theory. Not only that, but they have what seems to be a great deal of evidence—police reports, interviews, timelines. Stuart's killing did, according to the show and as Max's family hypothesized all those years before, have to do with drugs. A dealer expanding his reach from the near suburbs to the farther ones collided with Stuart, who was pushing his own small business outside of Schaumburg. Threats and demands were made. Warnings given.

Most incredibly, the producers have unearthed witnesses, according to whom Stuart was snatched from the Denny's parking lot, forced into the back of a black Chevy Lumina. No one saw him again until his body was discovered. How did this escape the police? Max feels the anger of his parents. Who was it that didn't ask, didn't see, didn't care?

Then, from the penultimate episode of Stuart's *Storyline*, a man named Craig Tulley:

Tulley: We took him to that house. Nobody lived there yet, so it was perfect. There weren't even lights in the streets. So we pulled through with just our fog lights on.

Producer: Who was driving?

Tulley: It was either this kid Josh or this kid Majid. Both of them were there for sure, but I can't remember who was driving. I was in the back. Me and Randall. We had the kid between us.

Producer: The kid was Stuart Shelenberg.

Tulley: Yeah. I didn't do shit to that kid once we were in the house. That's the truth. I want that known. That shit was all Randall and the other two. I was like a lookout. I didn't touch that kid. You can check the DNA and whatever else, man, I didn't get near that kid.

Producer: But you didn't help him either.

[silence]

Producer: Did you know what was going to happen to him?

Tulley: I knew he was going to get the shit beat out of him. He was snatching buyers from Randall, and Randall wasn't going to stand for that. Far as I knew, Randall told him to back the fuck off and get his business elsewhere. That's what I was told. Kid didn't listen. Did I know he was going to get a bullet in the head? No. I don't even know why it happened, honestly. It's not like the kid was going to be back on Randall's turf after the beating he got. He was small-time. No way he would have kept on after that night.

Producer: So who pulled the trigger?

Tulley: I don't know.

Producer: You were there.

Tulley: I went and had a cigarette.

Producer: In the middle of all this you left to smoke a cigarette?

Tulley: That's the truth. Next thing I know there's the shot. None of those guys ever told me who done it and I sure as hell wasn't going to ask. We just left.

Tulley speaks from the Illinois State Penitentiary in Quincy, Illinois, where he is serving a life sentence for the murder of a convenient store cashier, and his participation in the program is, in part, meant to curry favor in a bid to reduce his sentence. The other part, he says, is that he wanted to tell the truth.

And why hasn't he told it before?

"Nobody ever asked until now."

· · · ·

On Friday that week, two days before the final show airs, one of the producers calls Max at work. She tells Max that they need to talk, and Max leaves the office to go to his car. While he crosses the parking lot, the producer brings Sandy in on a conference call. It is snowing again and the windows are covered and the light inside the car is ethereal and unearthly.

"Sandy, are you there?" the producer says.

"Yes." Her voice sounds thin and nervous. Unlike her.

"Max?"

"I'm here," he says.

"Good. We're calling you both now because we want you to know what's going on before the final show posts. We need to tell you that this morning the police have made four arrests in Stuart's murder."

"Oh my god," Sandy says.

"This Randall person?" Max says. He feels oddly detached. Not how he thought he might in his many fantasies of this moment. Now, he only wants the information. He recalls his parents: *They need to tell us more. . . .*

"Yes," the producer says.

"And the other two in the car."

"Yes. And another man who was involved but not there physically that night."

"And Craig Tulley?"

"It looks like he'll be charged also."

"But he'll get a reduction for the other killing."

"That's up to the Illinois Attorney General. I don't have anything more than that."

"This is unbelievable," Sandy says.

"We don't know what will happen now," the producer says, "but, yeah, it's really more than we ever hoped for." A chirp of laughter escapes her throat.

After the phone call, Max calls his sister back.

"Hey," she says.

"Hey."

And he hears her begin to cry and he cries himself and they cry together into their phones for a good long time before Sandy finally sniffles and says, "Ok," and Max says, "Yeah," and Sandy says, "I'll call you later."

· · · ·

It is another year before the trial. Though Max goes to Chicago, the night before it begins, he and Sandy decide not to attend. Sandy suggests it, but Max easily agrees. The prosecuting attorney is not pleased. "I cannot overestimate the effect your presence could have," he tells Max. But there is no dissuading them. Now that they've made the decision to sit the trial out, he cannot believe they were going to go in the first place. What he'd imagined as some kind of triumphant catharsis now seems to him a child's fantasy, and he realizes that he was a child when he first conceived it.

Instead, they go to the cemetery where Stuart and their parents are. The dry air is bitterly cold. Both Max and Sandy wear the latest gear from Max's company, but it's still cold.

"How often you get out here?" Max asks.

"Every couple weeks."

"You really come here every couple weeks?"

Sandy looks over at him.

He says, "I don't know if I would. After all these years."

"I mean, obviously I do it for me. I do it because it helps me in some way. Sometimes it's just to get out of the house. 'I'm going to the cemetery' shuts everybody up *tout suite*."

"It's still good of you."

She points to a bare tree a couple dozen yards away. "That's a maple and when the leaves are on it's got this great sound when the wind comes through. I like to stand under it."

"Just listening to it?"

"Yeah."

"How long do you stand there?"

"A couple hours," Sandy says.

"Seriously?"

"No. Idiot. A few minutes. It's peaceful."

Max flies back to Colorado just four days into the trial. The news people and other followers anticipate a quick guilty verdict. The evidence, most of it collected by the producers at *Storyline*, is exhaustive and damning. So much so that Max must force himself away from a swelling anger over its not having been amassed back when the crime was fresh. In the course of the trial the local police are called to the stand again and again. The underlying question each time: How did you miss this? And this? And this?

The jury deliberates for thirty-six hours and returns to the courtroom with the verdict predicted. One of the producers from *Storyline*, present at the trial, calls Max, who has stayed home from work in anticipation. The words soak into him. He holds his hands to his face. He calls Sandy. He ignores a half dozen calls from numbers he does not know. He opens a window and feels the frigid air blast through his clothes to his skin. He feels as if he has been drugged. The world is odd and unfamiliar. The colors of the walls and the curtains and the snow outside have all shifted ever so slightly. He issues nonsense shouts and chirps into the room. "Oww," he calls sharply. "Oww, oww." He feels not quite human. Like something incorporeal. And yet there he is.

In the midst of all this, what brings the name to mind? Something his eye swept across? Some noise registered below his consciousness? Whatever it was, he finds himself snapped back to the world and logged onto Facebook for the first time in more than a year, typing "Andrés Herrera." The page is still there, just as Max remembers.

Nothing has been heard from him.

No one has seen him.

This page is for people who loved Andrés.

Max checks his phone. There they are—the stilted scripted voicemails from so long ago. He listens to each once, and then over again. The boy's voice, his careful articulation of the words. Max can nearly hear the held breath of his elders surrounding him. He thinks he can feel, in the silences between Mateo Herrera's words, the presence of the boy's aunt and uncle, Andrés's mother and father.

His mood alights into a manic high. He redials the *Storyline* producer. He bounces in place.

"I have your next thing," Max says.

"Thing?"

"Your next series. I've got it. Oh my god, it's perfect. There's a man named Andrés Herrera and he disappeared in Mexico, somewhere near Juárez. It's probably the cartels. They took him. You can do this. You can go back and track what happened." He is nearly breathless with excitement.

The producer is quiet. Then, "Was he involved with them? The cartels?"

"No. I don't know. Could be. They took him, though. His family is looking for him. I have phone numbers for them. You can call them."

"I'm just . . ." the producer starts. "I'm sure there are hundreds of people who go missing. I'm just wondering what's special about this guy."

"What was special about Stuart?"

"Well, the first thing about your brother was that it felt like it might be a good story. White kid in the suburbs, et cetera. Not to put too fine a point on it."

Max feels a familiar something weighing on his chest. That old shame.

He hangs up the phone.

Andrés Herrera will never be found. Max is certain of this. This man, someone's child, someone's god, is already dead, his desiccated body somewhere in the desert, the skin and muscle and fat long ago consumed and shat out by whatever birds and animals and bugs happened upon it. He is as dead as Max's brother. There will be no finding Andrés Herrera, though. And no one will ever be made to answer for his death. There will be no justice in the case of his murder, no surprise twist in the plot. He will only be lost and grieved and then, not too many years hence, he will be very simply dead and forgotten.

Julia and Nora come home, and Julia stands in the doorway of Max's office, says, "Well?" and Max tells her about the verdict. Julia cries, and this gets Max going. Through the prism of his tears he sees out the window that it is snowing again. Always, always, so much snow.

Nora comes in and sees her parents crying. She says, "What's wrong?" and before either of them can answer, her own face crumbles. The whole family crying now. Max sniffles and wipes his nose with his sleeve, says, "Nothing's wrong." He lifts her small body up onto his lap, and she presses her face into his shoulder. "Everything's fine," he says into her hair, like a child's song. "Everything's fine, everything's fine, everything's fine."

INTERLUDE

NESTS

· · · ·

My mother would tell me our old live oak could predict the weather. "Sweetie," she'd say to me out on our porch. "You watch those squirrel nests once it starts getting cold, see where they are on the branches. Far out toward the ends, no worries. Close in toward the trunk, you better hunker down and order an extra cord of wood. It's gonna be a long one."

My brothers were never with us. Or if they were, they'd roll their eyes and spin on their heels, then head inside to play video games or study, the both of them dead set on med school, on getting as far away from home as possible. But I'd stay out with our mom, listen to her talk about how the world tells us things if only we bother to hear it.

Now, older and outvoted, I watch the excavators and claws, near-elemental in their power, take down the porch, the shelter beyond. The shed and bushes and trees. And I wonder what will be in that spot where the oak was, what corner of what row of new and flimsy houses. What laundry room will whisper of the winters to come.

THREE

SOMEONE INTERESTING I KNOW
An Interview with My Uncle Chris by Sadie Fenton

· · · ·

On October 9, my mom drove me up to Louisville so I could interview my Uncle Chris. He lives in a red brick house. All over the house there are pictures of my cousin Sonny and still a few pictures of my Aunt Margot, even though they got divorced. There is also a lot of stuff for rock climbing, like ropes and these hook things. His house has a deck by some woods, and Uncle Chris said we should sit out there while we talked. He drank coffee and made me a smoothie with blueberries and some other berries I forgot the name of and protein powder, which wasn't as bad as I thought it would be. Here is what we talked about.

[Mom's note: The conversation ended up going much longer than we had anticipated, Mrs. Perez, and there is really no way Sadie would be able to transcribe the whole thing in time, so I'm doing the typing.]

Sadie Fenton: Thank you for agreeing to talk to me.
Uncle Chris: Well, you're very welcome, sweet girl. Or I guess I shouldn't call you 'sweet girl.' We'll keep it professional.
SF: Ok.
UC: How's that smoothie?
SF: It's good.
UC: Good.

[Mom's note: As I understand this assignment, it is to be done in stages with the editing coming later, is this correct? Under this understanding, I'm not editing anything out. Obviously there are some things here that will not be in the final version she turns in and presents to the class. I hope this is what you're looking for. If not, it is my fault, not Sadie's. ☺]

SF: Can you tell me about what your life was like when you were a kid?

UC: It was . . . hmm, that's a big question. Well, you know I grew up here in Bardstown with your mother and Grandma and Grandpa. We had a good life, I guess, basically. Never wanted for anything essential. You know, it was a small town, so once I was a teenager it felt a little stifling. But when I was younger it was mostly fine. I spent a lot of time by myself. I'm much older than your mother, you know. I was already twelve by the time she came along.

SF: What did you do to have fun when you were younger?

UC: A dangerous question. I don't want to give you any ideas.

SF: Ok.

UC: No, I'm joking. Honestly, I don't know what I did before climbing. All that's kind of a blur. I think I watched a lot of tv. But then I started exploring all the forests around there. It became my escape from the tension between my parents. They weren't always the happiest people. They got married and had me young and never seemed to forgive the world for allowing them to make that decision. Money was tight and there was some arguing. So my buddies and I would hitch or beg rides from Bardstown out to the forest a few miles away, spending all day tromping around and racing each other to the top of the old fire lookout. When we got our driver's licenses, we drove out to Tioga Falls near Fort Knox. Sometimes there'd be military exercises that we'd watch from a distance. That's when I started climbing, pulling myself up dried-out waterfalls and seeing how far I could get moving horizontally across mossy old stone retaining walls. And then I started hitting the climbing gyms here in Louisville. Challenges made sense to me. I liked being a physical body. Do you know what I mean?

SF: I think so.

UC: It's like, we spend so much time in our heads, or creating whatever persona we want the world to see . . .

[silence]

UC: This isn't all that fascinating, is it? Should we just jump to your cousin Sonny? I feel like that's the thing maybe you want to hear about.

SF: Um . . .

UC: It's fine. His story is a lot more interesting than mine. He's been on tv and in magazines and stuff.

SF: Ok, sure.

[Mom's note: Sonny's also been written about in books and was a big part of a documentary that came out a few years ago, him and Matty both.]

UC: Good, ok. The first thing you ought to know is that he wasn't born with the ability to climb. In fact, quite the opposite. When he was little, he was afraid of heights. I would have to hold him by the waist as he climbed the fragile little dogwood out in front of our house. Only a foot and a half off the ground and his limbs would shake the leaves. He would get up to the first juncture before asking to be helped down. So I'd put a hand on his shoulder, and I remember marveling at how tiny it was, this piddly knob that seemed no bigger than my thumb knuckle. He would be disappointed in himself and cry. God, how I worried about him. So hard on himself. But then, an hour later, he'd be back outside, a hand on the lowest branch, saying "Daddy," and I would understand and go to him. In the few interviews I've given about him and Matty I've made a point of mentioning this stuff. I want people to understand the full extent of what he did, how hard he pushed himself. But I also want people to know what it was that made him so great. There's one thing you need to be a climber, to climb higher than you climbed the day before and still be safe—or relatively safe. Do you know what that is?

SF: Ropes?

UC: Well, yes, you do need ropes. But I'm talking about something inside of you.

SF: Courage!

UC: You need courage, absolutely. But there's something you need even more than that. Do you want me to tell you what it is? It's fear. Even more than being brave, you have to be afraid. You have to be scared of falling, more than you're scared of anything else in the world. Your fear says that you understand what you're doing, that you respect the rock and you respect gravity. That's the first thing I ever taught Sonny about climbing. Don't ever lose that fear.

SF: He started climbing with you?

UC: Yes. If you ask Sonny's mother, I am the one to blame.

SF: Aunt Margot doesn't like rock climbing?

UC: Your aunt Margot doesn't like her son putting himself in mortal danger as a hobby. I can't say I blame her.

[silence]

UC: Your cousin didn't have an easy childhood. Aunt Margot and I did what we could to counter the pain that finds a kid who is small and different, but I guess it's the fate of all parents to face the vast depth of their failures. We didn't protect him as well as we would have liked.

[silence]

UC: Hey, how are you doing, anyway? I should have asked.

SF: Ok.

UC: Yeah? You talk to your dad lately?

SF: Not really.

UC: You know if you ever need anything, you just let me know.

[silence]

UC: So. Sonny. When he started climbing, he just became . . . I don't want to say a different person, but it was like the best parts of him inflated, you know. Got bigger. The parts of him that were smart and brave and funny. And the other things kind of receded. I saw him interact with the other climbers at the gym with such ease. I watched him get stronger, his body changing. This was, what, nearly twenty years ago he started? And I still remember slowly coming to the understanding that climbing was different for Sonny than it ever had been for me. For me it was always about the fun. It was about the view from the top and the physical exhaustion and the pleasure of pizza and beers an hour later. For him, though . . . I don't know . . . it was like he was climbing toward something I couldn't see. And then Matty came along.

SF: How did they meet?

UC: Sonny and I were on a climbing trip in Yosemite. Sonny was twenty-one, I guess. Matty maybe a year older. It was early evening and we were done for the day, Sonny and I. We'd already gone up Southeast Face that day and Blind Man's Bluff the day before. These are pretty challenging faces, and I could barely lift my arms. And there was Matty sitting on a rock nearby, coiling his rope, and he said hey to Sonny. I could see the attraction between them. I'm telling you, it was electric blue. They started talking, and Matty said it was cool that we did this together, said his own dad didn't talk to him since he came out five years before. You know what gay is, right?

SF: Yes. My friends and me are starting an alliance group.

UC: You are? At your age? That's . . .

[silence]

UC: I'm sorry. I . . .

[silence]

UC: You kids are going to make this world so much better than it's ever been before.

[silence]

UC: Anyway . . . sorry. Ok, Sonny invited Matty to climb the Phoenix with us the next day. The day after that, when Sonny and I were in our hotel room packing up to fly back home, he said he might see if he could change his flight and stay another couple days to keep climbing. I knew Matty had another couple climbs on his itinerary. I understood and said it was no problem and called the airline myself. It was only after Sonny got home to Louisville that he let slip that they went up Book of Job, a grade three ascent I never would have let him climb had we been together. I was so mad.

I've climbed harder, he said.

No, you haven't, I told him. You literally haven't.

Well, I could, he said. I can.

And of course he was right. And Matty just elevated his talents. He gave Sonny something I never could—a sense of a natural place in the world. God, how my boy flourished. And I believe it was the same for Matty. This was no one-way deal. They came together like two parts of one beautiful new being.

They moved to L.A., into this minuscule little bungalow in a place called Echo Park. They were poor. You know what ramen is? It's this really cheap noodle thing. They ate lots of that. Los Angeles is a lot more expensive than Kentucky. I think they had fun, though, and they didn't seem to mind struggling. They saved up for trips to White River and Zion and the Gunks. That's what it was all about. When they were able to come back to Kentucky for visits, we all tripped out to the Gorge, where I was soon forced to fully accept my humble abilities. They were so much better than I could ever be. I sweated up faces that were just warm-ups for the boys. The one time I did try to lead, I took a nasty whipper that dropped me fifteen feet and left me banging against the rock. Bruised me up pretty good. After that I did my best to check my pride and stay on the ground.

[Mom's note: They even took Sadie and me out there once, and I can attest to the boys' abilities. I couldn't believe this was the same little boy who used to hide behind his parents' legs when even I came to visit. Somehow they convinced me to try a climb. My arms shook, but Sonny and Matty called out, "You got this, Auntie!" (Even Matty called me Auntie, though I was only nine years older than them.) After I got down they showed me pictures they'd taken on their phones. I was only about four feet off the ground! This was right around the first time Sadie's dad left, and I guess for that reason it was such a release for her and I to laugh, even if it was at my expense. But the boys didn't laugh. Instead they both talked about how scared they'd been their first times out, about how they still got scared. Sweet kids. And then I watched them go up these huge rock faces like spiders, hundreds of feet above us. A crowd gathered to watch. No one had seen anything like them.]

UC: They did some deep-water soloing—that's climbing without any ropes on cliffs over bodies of water in case of a fall. Sonny told me this was the only soloing they ever did, that they never went without ropes over land, but I suspected he was keeping something from me. Obviously I would have exploded. Soloing is dangerous and, honestly, pretty stupid. You have to promise me that if you ever want to climb, you'll come to me first and you'll never solo.

SF: I won't.

UC: Most of the time they were smart. Model climbers, really. And they were getting even better. They were together two years when they took on Fortress of Solitude in Colorado, a feat that got them profiled in both *Climbing* and *The Advocate*. A year later they summited El Capitan, which, I don't know if you know, but that's the big daddy. People dream of going up that rock. And after they did it, things got crazy. YouTube channels were dedicated to their climbs. The *New York*

Times Magazine did a whole thing on them. Nike approached them about sponsorship—an offer they turned down for some reason I never got to the bottom of. They went on *The Tonight Show*, sat there on a couch with a woman who played a superhero in some movies. Do you remember that? She was like, "You dudes are crazy, man." It was so strange. Like watching some other version of the world unfold right there in front of you.

[Mom's note: Sadie still talks about this. We drove up to Louisville and gathered at Chris's house and I let Sadie stay up late to watch it. I don't know that I've ever been so nervous in my life, even though all we were doing was sitting there looking at a tv. But I guess we never really lose the memory of who people were when they were young, and no matter what Sonny did, he would always be that fragile little boy I knew decades before.]

UC: The climbing community provided plenty of pushback, of course. Voices of dissent. People who seemed to love nothing more than to get on social media or write letters to the editor and point out the many men and women who accomplished all Sonny and Matty had and more, yet never received a mention in this or that magazine, let alone an invite to *The Tonight Show*. But the fact is that at every opportunity Sonny and Matty talked about those who came before and those who were out there every day taking on new rocks and defining new lines on old ones. They were students of climbing, and I don't think they ever claimed to be anything more than what they were. Two damn good climbers.

Of course, all that attention wasn't just because they were great climbers—they were, but there *are* plenty of those. It *did* have to do with them being a gay couple in a sport that isn't particularly known for that. Even the boys would admit this. But it was also that they were funny and handsome and incredibly charming, and this, along with their strength, was what made them so completely magnetic. They made people smile. In the face of a nearly constant onslaught of darkness all over the world, they were a picture of strength and love and triumph. I don't think I'm overstating the matter. The world needed Sonny and Matty. I really believe that.

SF: When did it happen with Matty?

[Mom's note: Even though I suspect this is the end of the story as far as Sadie's assignment goes, Mrs. Perez, I feel it is important not to simply cut off here. I worry about what kind of message that sends to Sadie. We can't deny the tragedies and hardships in our lives. How would that help equip Sadie for the next one to come along? Anyway, that's what I'm thinking now. We're all just trying to figure it out, moment to moment, aren't we?]

UC: About a year later, after the thing on tv and all that. They were out in Red Rock Canyon in Nevada, on a climb called Transcendence. Those rocks out there can be crumbly after a rain, just really fragile. I mean, everybody takes a whipper every once in a while. It's not a huge deal. You get a little bang when the rope catches, get slammed against the rock a bit, but then you reset. So I imagined Sonny didn't think too much of it, probably just a little start. Matty would just have to catch up. But I guessed one of his anchors didn't hold, or maybe a 'biner failed, and he just . . .

[silence]

UC: Honestly, I didn't really know what happened.

[silence]

UC: I got a call from someone at the hospital in Vegas. Sonny was fine. Matty hung on for a while, but was gone by the time I got there.

[silence]

UC: I went back to L.A. with Sonny and stayed for about a week. Margot was there, too, the both of us trying to get him to eat, trying to get him to talk. Not about what happened—just anything besides telling us he wasn't hungry or that he didn't want to talk. I would have stayed longer, but he didn't want us there anymore. Or at least that's what he said. A big part of me said I should stay anyway, no matter what he said. He's my son and he was in so much pain. Your aunt and I talked about it on this little back porch their house had. But in the end we decided to do as he wished.

Then, two months later, Sonny called and said he was going to climb Transcendence again.

No, I said. You're not.

But he insisted.

With who? I asked him. You can't do it alone.

It's not even tough, he said in a way that told me he wasn't really talking to me. It's such a simple climb, he said.

Sonny, no, I said, as if I could still tell him what to do. You shouldn't even be thinking about this.

We did climbs ten times harder than that one, he said.

You're not thinking right. Just slow down. Take a year.

I'm thinking fine, he said. I can climb it alone, but I was kind of wondering if you'd be up for it.

I was shocked and thought maybe I had misunderstood him. Me? I said. No. No way.

I'm going in April, before the winds kick up, he told me.

April? I said. It was only two months away. I can't be ready by April.

I listened to him breathe three thousand miles away. It was almost like I could hear a little smile rise on his face. So you *do* want to do it, he said.

Of course I did.

SF: And you went?

UC: That evening I ran eight miles and then booked myself a ticket to Vegas and another for Sonny from LAX. He'd been in magazines and on tv, but most of the time he was still a broke twenty-eight-year-old working at a climbing gym. Your mother never told you about this?

SF: We didn't talk much about Sonny and Matty after it happened.

[Mom's note: I could have done better, I know. We were on our own for real by then and I was just so tired.]

UC: Well, yeah, I went out there and met Sonny. We stayed at this really ridiculous place called the New York, New York that has a roller coaster going up over the building.

SF: Really?

UC: Yeah, it went right up outside my window. I checked in a bit before Sonny got there and watched all these people go whooshing past me, all of them screaming and smiling. It's a weird place, Vegas.

So then we went to run some trails at this spot called Bootleg Canyon. Sonny went ahead of me, as he always had since he hit puberty. I watched his New Balances push off the dirt like they were just barely making contact. Such a graceful runner, that kid. Right from the beginning he had that concentration that makes a good runner and a good climber. Sonny won all of the cross-country meets in high school. There were boys a year or two younger who would openly talk about how they couldn't wait for him to graduate so they might have a chance at coming in first once in a while. You know he went to Georgetown on scholarship and set records. I've still never seen anyone run like Sonny. But it was always climbing he wanted to do. That was his real love.

We went ten miles out, stopped and drained half of the water in our camelbacks, then turned around. By the time we got back to our rental car, I felt like I was melting. You ever feel that? Those noodle legs? So I'm pretty much collapsing, and Sonny's there scrambling up a boulder to have a last look around. Energy to spare.

And he calls to me, What's the line in that movie?

Which movie? I say.

Lawrence of Arabia, he says. There's that part where the guy asks him why he likes the desert.

Because it's clean, I said.

You should tell your mom to show you that when you get a little bigger. It's a great movie.

Later, we went to our rooms, showered and dressed, and went to the Strip. That's the main part of Vegas. We had an insanely expensive but delicious dinner, and I sat there luxuriating in Sonny's presence. I could look at him for hours, even then, nearly thirty years after his birth. My beautiful baby boy.

We sat there for a while, not talking, and then he says to me, Stop looking at me, Dad.

No, I told him.

It would be like telling me not to drink water or blink or something.

A grin—the first I'd seen since arriving—lifted his face, just for a second.

Our climb was the next morning, and he said he wanted to be in the car before sunup, heading out to the canyon. Ok, I told him, but as soon as I said it, something clicked in my brain. Like I just woke up from a dream.

I can't climb that rock, I said. There was no way. It was bigger than anything I'd ever done and I was way out of shape. I don't know what I was thinking. I won't make it to the top, I said.

You might, he said casually.

No, I said. I'm telling you, I'm not. Who are we kidding?

You're just getting nervous, he said.

Honey, listen to me, I said. I'm going to say something and you tell me if it sounds right: your father is going to summit Transcendence tomorrow morning. Does that sound even remotely possible to you? *Me?* Are we delusional?

No, he said. Then he let out a loud breath and looked toward the kitchen. Remember when you used to help me up that little tree in our front yard? he said.

The dogwood, I said.

Yeah, he said. The dogwood.

This isn't a dogwood tree, honey, I said.

And he looked at me and said, I know. That's what I'm saying. He finally looked me in the eyes. Of course you're not going to make it to the top. Jesus Christ, I don't even know if *I'll* make it all the way. But now that everything's dried out, the first half should be cake, so you'll do that and head back down and I'll keep on going.

I didn't know if I was mad at myself for my limitations or him for recognizing those limitations better than I could, or just embarrassed at having indulged in such an obvious fantasy. So you knew already? I said. This has been the plan?

And he says to me, I don't need you to hold me up anymore. I just wanted my dad here.

[silence]

SF: Are you ok?

UC: Yeah, I'm ok. And I'm almost done, I promise.

[silence]

UC: There weren't many people out yet in the canyon, and no one else at Transcendence, just Sonny and I. The rock was solid. Dry. Perfect. And it was a great route. Nice wide hand cracks. Big footholds. We made it up a couple hundred feet in no time. Man, I hadn't been out in so long. I mean, not in a gym, really out there feeling the breeze and the sun, chalking my hands and pulling myself up hold by hold. In bed the night before I had let myself entertain thoughts of actually making it to the top, but once we got there and I saw that big son of a gun rising up into the sky I knew it wasn't going to happen. But I made it farther than I thought I could. Sonny started calling down, You all right? And then at about three-fifty he started shouting, Ok, that's probably high enough! But I kept going. I was higher than I'd ever been. I couldn't even believe it. God, I hope you find something in your life that makes you feel like I felt that morning. You know the world so well up there. You feel your connection to everything else that has ever existed. It isn't about conquering the rock. Not at all. It's about understanding that you are the rock and the rock is you and you are every person on earth and every person is you and our existence is both finite and infinite at the same time. And up there you get it. It only lasts a second, but it all clicks in a way that changes you forever.

So we were at about four hundred feet and I realized that Sonny had stopped and I was right under him. I could see he had a good foothold; he didn't seem to be in trouble. So I just waited. And finally he called down, This is where it happened.

I glanced down and tried not to imagine the sensation Matty must have felt. The free fall. The terror. The confusion when he thought the rope should catch.

And then after a few seconds Sonny said to me, We were soloing.

My heart fell. How could they have been so stupid? How could he have forgotten the one most important thing I ever taught him—never lose your fear? But somewhere in me I'd known this was a possibility, and I knew it hadn't been the first time. I would ask about trips they took, and they'd get all cagey about answering. I don't know whose idea this particular one was, but even if it had been Matty's, they made their decisions together. Sonny should have said no. If they were being reckless, that was on the both of them. And Sonny knew that. My mind attempted to conceive of the guilt he must have been feeling all those months.

After another minute, Sonny called out, Ok, Dad. And I knew my climb was done. He hoisted himself up to the next anchor. I watched him test it once, twice, and keep going. It occurred to me that he might unhook and try to solo to the top, some guilt-driven dramatic gesture. But he didn't. Thank god. After a few minutes watching him get farther and farther away, I started lowering myself down.

I was at the base and Sonny still had another five hundred feet to go. I watched him the whole way. And you know what?

SF: What?

UC: He made it. Pulled himself right up over the top. And I saw him standing there at the edge, so tiny from where I was.

[silence]

UC: After the trip he told your aunt Margot and then spoke to Matty's parents, told them what really happened. And it's all going to come out tonight. That's the reason I'm telling you this. It'll be out and Sonny will face a lot of questions from the little sliver of the world that cares about such things. I'd rather you heard it from me. Should be a lot different from the last time he was on tv.

[silence]

UC: Anyway. I haven't climbed since that day on Transcendence.

SF: Are you ever going to?

UC: I really don't know, sweet girl. Maybe I'm too scared now. Maybe I'm scared of getting sad. Do you ever feel that way?

[silence]

SF: Sometimes my dad calls and it just makes it worse. So when Mom's phone rings I kind of hope it isn't him.

[silence]

SF: She's going to be here soon.

UC: Yeah, I guess so. Are there other questions you wanted to ask?

SF: No. . . . Well, there are, but they seem stupid now. There's a whole list we had to come up with in class. Like, what's your favorite food and do you have a favorite sports team.

UC: Those aren't stupid questions. But maybe you could call me, and we could go over anything else you want. And when Sonny gets back home from New York, maybe you can get him to answer a few, too. I think he's going to be around for a while. How would that be?

SF: Ok.

UC: He's the interesting one, after all.

[Mom's note: Mrs. Perez, I know this probably isn't what you were looking for in this assignment. It isn't what I expected, either. It occurs to me that Sadie might be better off starting over and interviewing someone else, like our neighbor with the seven Dalmatians or the woman at church who makes chocolate sculptures. But I'm not sure. What do you think? Should we keep plugging away and see what we can make of it? Do we even have a choice at this point?]

WE'VE GOT TONIGHT

. . . .

Outside Amanda Courtenay's wake, people smoked cigarettes and heaved arms around one another while Hank Margolis weaved through the cluster, his head down. The sun, high and blinding, washed out the details of the world. After nine hours of air travel (Dublin to Amsterdam, Amsterdam to Chicago), and two hours in the company of his ex-girlfriend's body, Hank's mind was not right. He moved forward on inertia, and now, turning the final corner to his apartment on Wolcott Avenue, an apartment he hadn't been to in over four months, he thought he might even fall, not make it those last three blocks. He envisioned his couch, his bed. He hoped, as he had many times since he first flew out of O'Hare for Dublin back when the air was springtime cool, that he hadn't left anything in the fridge to rot.

He could just see his building when he passed a man to whom he wouldn't have paid any mind had he not, even in his woozy, exhausted state, caught a glimpse of the man's azure eyes. They were set above taut high-boned cheeks, and below the stiff brim of a black baseball cap. But the eyes. That was easy.

"Chase," he said, turning to the man, now past.

The man stopped and looked, those eyes now in the shadow of his cap.

"Hank fuckin' Margolis," he said in the lilting North Carolina drawl that thrust a whole history of acquaintance back to the forefront of Hank's mind. He was thin, half of what he'd been in college fifteen years before when the two of them swung in the same circles, a mere wire hanger beneath a long-sleeved black tee and wide-legged black pants, the sort with buckles dangling from the seams—the sort that Malcolm McLaren, back in the day, would have called *bondage trousers*.

"I'm standing here, I'm seeing you, but it all seems like a mirage," Chase said.

"I know just what you mean," Hank said.

Hank switched his valise to his left hand and extended his right. Chase Bonnay took it and tossed his other arm around Hank's shoulder. He smelled of cigarettes, sweat, and something pungently chemical. His skin, up close, was blotched red and stippled with tiny whiteheads.

"Look at you, man," Chase said, flicking a finger into the lapel of Hank's suit jacket. "What'd you just get back from, an asshole convention?" His mouth spread into the sly smile that Hank now recalled as a nearly permanent fixture of Chase's demeanor. He'd been the sort of young man who could insult the biggest, baddest motherfucker at a party and receive only a fresh beer in return. Surely part of it was his accent, which oozed sweetly amidst the midwestern mumblings of their Indiana college town. He'd brought girls home who, on the surface, shouldn't have given him a glance. He'd charmed extra half grades from professors. But now that grin was disrupted by a grill of rot: the teeth behind Chase's lips were chipped and blackened around the edges, piss-yellow everywhere else.

"A wake," Hank said with a shrug, a note of apology in his voice.

"Oh, well, shit," Chase said. "Friend?"

Hank nodded.

"Man," Chase said with two shakes of his head. Then, "You stay around here?"

Hank hesitated. He didn't know this man anymore, and he looked desperate. But in its fatigued state his mind could not conjure anything but the truth.

"Right here." He pointed to his building.

"You know what this is, you being here?" Chase said. "This is God's will or some shit that I run into you on this spot right here. This is fate. See, I'm in a little bit of a situation. No, I know, but listen, I'm not asking for money or anything. I'm not a bum, man. You know me."

"Ok," Hank said skeptically.

"I just need a couple hours. I need a place to stay for just a couple hours. You got a couple hours you can spare me? I don't need anything else. Just a place to sit down and chill for a little bit."

"You going to tell me why?"

"It's not that. I'm not on the lam or anything."

Hank normally would have then excused himself with some story of business begging for attention. Certainly he'd run into old friends before at bars and grocery stores and, like now, on the street, but he'd never had much interest in rekindling the relationships beyond quick hellos and vague catch-ups. The past was the past, and so on. And he'd long since lost any desire to court the brand of squalor with which Chase, based on his appearance, seemed to be intimately attached. As he aged, Hank's tolerance for crazy and broken plummeted. But it was a strange day already, a day against which Hank had no energy to fight.

"Come on up," he said.

• • • •

The air in his apartment was dead—hot and hanging with rank dampness, as if each molecule had been breathed in and out a hundred times already. The shades were down, and with his eyes not yet adjusted from the blinding light outside, the living room was nearly obliterated in his vision. He felt for the entryway light and flipped the switch.

"I've been out of town," Hank said to Chase, who'd come in silently behind him.

There was an austere stillness to this collection of rooms, a silence that was only momentarily broken by the clatter of plastic blinds as Hank yanked the cords, allowing a cascade of light to wash through the windows. With some difficulty, he jerked the window sash up. A burst of air coughed into the room.

Chase sat on the couch, leaned his head back, and worried the brim of his cap. "Let me see if I have anything to drink," Hank said, though he knew he didn't; he'd cleaned his kitchen out completely before leaving for Ireland. He hoped he'd at least left some ice in the trays, but found them empty and upside down on their rack. The water spit and hacked from the tap a few moments, and Hank filled two glasses.

"Sorry," he said, handing a glass of lukewarm water to his old friend. "All I have right now."

Chase drank the entire glass down, a feat that left him breathless. "Where were you?"

"Dublin," Hank said. Then added, "Ireland."

"Yeah, man," Chase said. "I've heard of it."

"I'm teaching there for the year. Heading back tomorrow."

Hank had been invited to teach a series of courses in a program at Trinity College. A year of American Studies. Hank had plodded away in the discipline for nearly a decade before penning a book that had somehow gotten caught up in a tiny breeze within the cultural zeitgeist. *Songs of Ourselves: A History of Heartland Rock* chronicled the uber-American musical genre that peaked in the mid-80s but still remained—as Hank argued in the book—a touchstone for the nation's understanding of itself. Springsteen, Mellencamp, Petty, as well as those slightly less known: Lucinda Williams, John Hiatt. The Irish, it seemed, went wild for this crop of troubadours, and so it was natural that Hank was one of the handful of professors invited to participate in the program. And with a stalled follow-up book project—a history of New

York's little-known "No Wave" musical movement (his publisher was not thrilled)—he eagerly accepted the twelve-month distraction.

Hank lowered himself into an armchair across from where Chase sat, and they ran through a few general pleasantries of reunion. Hank told Chase a bit about his work, his research. He mentioned briefly a girl he'd begun seeing in Dublin (leaving out the fact that she was sixteen years his junior and a student at Trinity). They revisited old friends and antics, all the while Hank trying to not let his eyes roam too freely over the other man's ravaged face and teeth.

At Chase's request, Hank retrieved his book. "Hot shit," Chase said, perusing the back cover and inside flaps. "Check you out." Hank rolled his eyes at the thought of his author photo, all blue denim and white cotton. Aping the musicians inside.

Hank excused himself and went to his bedroom, even more stifling than the front room and kitchen. He opened the screenless window, which faced the brick wall of the building next door, just two feet away, and leaned his face into the relative cool. He retrieved his iPhone from his pocket and saw no missed calls, no voicemail. He tapped to his email account and found only a message from the literature department chair at Trinity wishing Hank safe travels and condolences on his loss. Hank had offered only cursory details about his abrupt departure, and he figured most of his colleagues would assume it had been a family member who died.

He took another moment to check Facebook and Twitter, but found no messages, no posts, no tweets of interest. He'd been hoping for something from Madeline, the woman—the *girl*, really—he'd been seeing the past two months. She was not his student; this Hank insisted on repeating to himself in one way or another nearly every time he saw or even thought of her. Yes, she was a student at the university, and no, she was not yet twenty-three (as compared to his thirty-eight), but she was not enrolled in his course and seemed to have zero interest in The Boss's oeuvre, so there was little chance she would opt into Hank's upcoming second and final semester. Yet his insistence on the academic legality of the relationship only served to confirm what he certainly already knew. There was a reason why he declined invitations to go out with her and her friends, why most of their dates were spent in bed.

But perhaps he wouldn't have to worry about it anymore. He checked again just to confirm. No messages, no posts, no tweets. When he'd seen her the day before (was it only the day before? Two days?) she rubbed the back of his head and cooed sympathetically in the bedroom of his flat. They'd just made love and were still mostly undressed. He'd just told her about Amanda's death and his need to return to the States.

"You were close then?" she asked.

"We were."

"When was the last time you saw her?" she said.

"A long time."

"Like, years?"

"Fifteen."

"*Fifteen*?" She stopped rubbing. No more cooing. "Sorry, I'm just surprised. You're flying all the way back to America to see a girl you haven't seen in fifteen years get buried."

"You don't understand," Hank said.

"Tell me," she said, bringing back a sweeter tone.

"No," he said. "It's pointless." He stood up from the bed, tugged on boxers and a t-shirt.

"Why's that?"

"Because you won't understand," he said. "Because you're a *child*." It wasn't the first time he'd gone after her for her age. His way of pushing her away, not too different from what he'd done to Amanda back in grad school. It was Amanda he thought of when he was with Madeline.

He saw her face, the pitying smile for the cliché he'd become: the horn-dog American prof bedding the student body abroad.

Madeline spun to the other side of the bed and pulled on her underwear. She shouted, "If I'm a child, then you're a pathetic fucking pedo." And without another word, she yanked on her jeans and shirt, hooked her Pumas with two fingers, and walked out. So it was no wonder, no surprise, that she hadn't reached out. His work done, she'd finally lost patience with him.

Hank returned to the living room to find Chase lying across the couch, thumbing through his book. "Seger, man," Chase said without looking up. "Fucking 'Night Moves,' right?"

Hank went to the kitchen and refilled Chase's water glass, set it back on the table.

"You should write a book about me, man," Chase said. "I'm playing music. It's like throwback techno, you know. The stuff we used to listen to in college. Remember those warehouse parties?"

"It was always more garage than warehouse," Hank said.

"You know, though. All that's coming back. Toss in a little old-school house." He set the book on the floor, sat up, and bobbed his head to an imaginary beat. "It's all coming back. People want to move. Enough of all this sad bastard music. Fucking hipsters playing ukuleles and singing about their beards."

Chase's story, when they got to it, was muddled and difficult for Hank to follow. Chase drummed open palms on his knees and his fingers on the coffee table while recalling a labyrinthine knot of people and events. He lived in Chicago at the moment, but at other points had stationed himself in Austin and Portland, in Omaha and Madison. He had even, it seemed—if Hank was following—returned to their Indiana college town, where he tended bar and spun records under the name DJ Jesus Fuck. He'd lost his parents within six months of each other. At some point he was robbed at gunpoint. At some point he was jumped and beaten. At multiple points he was arrested. It was impossible to keep a time line straight, so bestrewn was his monologue with stammering asides, references to stories not yet told and characters not yet introduced, and great leaps back and forth across years. But while the larger story eluded, each individual anecdote offered a small glimpse at the man.

"A couple years ago," he said, "I got caught trying to heist a Christmas tree. I come out of the Empty Bottle and I'm shithammered and there's this tree place. I haven't had a Christmas tree in years, man, twenty years probably, and I see them all propped up, man, and I'm like, *I want one*. You know? So I start climbing the fence but at the top my pants get caught up on the little belt hook thing. Right at the back, so I can't reach it. I twist and turn trying to unhook myself, but nothing doing. I'm stuck, man. So I'm just hanging there, arms crossed, waiting it out. Finally Chicago's finest pull up like I knew they would, and they look at me up there and kind of look at each other, and say to me, 'What are you doing up there, bud?' Stupid question, right? So I say, 'I was trying to steal a Christmas tree, the fuck do you think I'm doing up here?' I was in the can for three months."

"Three months?" Hank said. "For trying to steal a Christmas tree?"

Chase waved a dismissive hand. "Man, they found some shit on my person."

"Jesus," Hank said.

Chase shrugged and said, "Life."

A negligible breeze came through the window, offering a momentary respite from the heat. But just as quickly, it was gone.

"You want to tell me what's going on with you? Today, I mean." Hank said.

Chase leaned back further into the couch, passed a hand across his chapped face. "I'm going into a facility. Tonight. My aunt lives down in

Pilsen—she's coming to get me, but she can't do it until she's done with work. Not until like eight o'clock. I got a problem, man. Little this, little that. Mostly crystal, though. Bad shit, man, that shit. You ever? No good. It gets you, man. Gets you down in your core, you know. Eats away at you. I've done some shameful things on its behalf. So I'm going in, getting clean. I've been staying with a guy, but he's in deeper than me, you know. Needed to get away from that."

Chase's confession put an awkward current to the air between them. Neither seemed to know what to say next. Finally, Chase said, "So who was your boy? Cat whose funeral you were at. How'd he go?"

"She," Hank said.

"Oh," Chase said. "Fuck." As if to lose a man was one thing, but for a woman to die was something else entirely. A tragedy.

"It was—" Hank started, then paused. "It was suicide?" His voice formed the statement into a question, an apology. "Nobody said exactly how."

Chase lay back on the couch, staring at the ceiling. "I tried once," he said. "Pills. Along with a fifth of Polish vodka. Plastic jug kind. No good, though. Just woke up about a day later covered in puke. Shat myself. Pissed. Nasty business trying to die and living through it."

Hank marveled at this man's openness. He seemed to hide nothing. If there was any opacity to him, it was due to his trying to tell everything at once.

"She was my girlfriend in grad school," Hank said. "This was in Michigan. About three years we were together. Lived together most of that."

"Good gal?"

"She was great, yeah. Nice person. Really pretty. Smart. All that. We were pretty good, too. Used to take weekends out at those Michigan beach towns—Holland, Grand Haven. We were broke, but we'd make it happen. Didn't need much back then."

Chase watched him with those kind, icy eyes.

"She tried to do herself in twice while we were together. Pills both times. The first time it was like this crazy thing. She was like, 'I don't know what I was thinking.' We treated it more like a weird fluke than anything. Stupid."

Hank remembers thinking she was more shaken up by having tried suicide than anything that had made her try in the first place. Not that he knew just what had prompted the act. He supposed he didn't want to know, and he supposed she understood this. So they didn't talk much about it. Got on with their lives.

The second time she went into the hospital for a month.

"I cheated on her while she was in there," Hank said to Chase. "Can you believe that? Girlfriend's in the psych ward and I'm out running after tail like I'm sixteen."

"Long time ago," Chase said.

"It's hard being with someone who's sick. You start feeling sorry for yourself and getting resentful. You start thinking it's okay to do whatever you're doing."

He left her two months after she got out of the hospital. Those two months felt interminable—endless days and sleepless nights, never knowing what to say, what to do, always wanting something other than what his life was right then. But now he thinks of such a period as nothing. A blip. Things get busy, it can take him two months to read a book.

He recalled the way she sat on their couch, her hands in her lap, as if nothing out of the ordinary was happening. He held a floppy duffel bag full of clothes in his hand and moved toward the door. Amanda then lay on the couch, her face turned to the back. "It's going to be harder for you," she said without looking at him, "to love anyone. The longer you go without giving yourself to anyone, the harder it will be. And at some point you're going to realize that it isn't a choice anymore. You just won't have it in you."

Descending the stairs of what had been their building, he felt like he'd just been cursed, though he understood it was nothing of the sort. He just didn't like the way she knew him.

He stopped going out. Gave up his friends, his hangouts. He put himself into his work. During this time, Hank flourished as a scholar, bringing home departmental and university-wide awards for both his research and his teaching. In many ways, it was the best time of his life. He had few attachments; his work was rewarding and increasingly recognized. Then he was awarded a prestigious postdoc at Princeton. He didn't even move his furniture. And he didn't contact Amanda. He just left.

"What do they call that now?" he said. "Ghosting? I ghosted."

"You never saw her again?"

"Not until today."

Earlier in the day, he'd been surprised at how many people came to Amanda's wake. Over a hundred, he'd say, just in the hour he was there. He came to her corpse, looked at the makeup-caked face of the woman he'd lived with and abandoned. He thought back to Madeline's question: why would he come all this way after all this time? And he knew the answer. Because she was dead and she could no longer need him.

The two men sat in silence for a long time. The light outside peaked and then began to turn slowly toward day's end. Several times Hank found his thoughts caught between waking and dreaming. One moment he was thinking of Amanda or Madeline, and the next his mind was roaming wildly into nonsense. Whenever he came back to himself, he couldn't recall just where he'd been. He looked across the room at Chase, still sitting, eyes closed, every once in a while opening them and sipping from the water glass.

After some indeterminate time, Chase sat up agitatedly. Hank's eyes jolted open. Chase arched his back and rolled his head back and forth. He let out a high-pitched groan. "Starting to get the itch, man. What time is it?"

Hank checked his phone. Nearly eight. Still no messages. No posts. No tweets.

Chase rapped on the coffee table. "This is the bitch of it. Your body wants it so bad. Mind, too."

"You can hold out," Hank said.

"Don't suppose you got any blow."

Hank apologized.

"You just get so tired without it. Weed?"

"No," Hank said. "I don't think you're supposed to show up at rehab baked, anyway."

Chase smiled, an expression of ease momentarily overcoming his face. "Sure it happens, though, probably more often than not." He stood and shook out his limbs one by one. He languidly shadowboxed the wall. "I'm telling you, man, you should write a book on me. I got stories. Plus now I'm getting right with the Lord. Figuratively speaking."

"Maybe I will."

"Bestseller, sure enough, my brother. Everybody'll be like, no way this dude's for real. But here I am, real as anything. I'd be like, here's my Twitter handle, hit me up."

A faint buzzing came from Chase's heavily hanging pants. He snatched a flip phone from his pocket and read a text. He asked Hank his address and then transcribed it onto the keypad. "On her way, man. 'Round the corner."

"You did it."

"Gettin' right." He clapped his hands twice. "I'm telling you I'm not one for God and all that, but how else can I explain you coming down this street just at that moment?"

"Coincidence."

"You see it how you want."

Chase slapped Hank's hand, hugged him. He said, "You're a good guy, you know?"

"Where are you going to go after treatment?"

"Shit, I always got places to go," Chase said, but he didn't sound so sure of it. There was a nervousness in his voice and in the way he turned away and started once again to box the wall. Hank's mind roamed the rooms of the apartment where they stood, the rooms that would be empty for another eight months. What would that kind of time give this man? Yet he said nothing.

The building was shrouded in shadow by the time Chase ambled down the steps outside Hank's door, and Hank was alone in his apartment. He did not turn on any lights but settled himself onto the couch, still warm from Chase's body, and fell quickly asleep swathed in Chicago dusk.

When he woke to a car alarm sounding through the open window, it was just past midnight. Even with such a simple starting point, his groggy mind stumbled while calculating the time in Dublin. Too early to call, but he could email or message if he wanted to. He didn't. He went to the window and considered walking to a bar, fitting in a few drinks before last call, but instead he simply went to his bedroom, stripped, and slid himself between the musty sheets.

• • • •

Hank flew back to Dublin the next day. The day after that he broke it off with Madeline at a pub in Temple Bar overlooking the River Liffey. An asshole place to break up with someone, surrounded by raucous, red-cheeked students drunk on beer and youth and beauty, but he knew she wouldn't be devastated, only angry in a general way. Nothing specific

149

to their relationship. She called him a few names, raising her voice only slightly above the din of the pint bingers. When she seemed done, he apologized once more and left, knowing that she would stay at the pub and roar to friends, who would console her about this romantic inconvenience. With the exception of one afternoon tryst near the end of Hank's stay in the city, he and Madeline kept away from one another for the remainder of his time in Ireland.

The director of the program assured Hank that his classes had provided invaluable insight into America's depiction of itself, its self-formed mythology, and that he would be welcome back any time the opportunity arose. At the end of his final lecture at Trinity, his students applauded—something that had never happened before—and he was moved to wish that he could remain there, though he knew this was merely a preliminary stage of nostalgia. Before returning home, Hank boarded planes and trains and wandered the circuitous streets of Paris, Berlin, and Venice, speaking little, taking in the sights, a heartland American in the temporary role of the classic European flâneur.

He taught two classes at Northwestern the next fall, and another two in the spring, and was given the impression by the department head that a permanent position might be formed—a thought that simultaneously comforted and terrified him. Feeling too tired and old to continue the transient life, he knew he would apply for and take the job if offered, but some part of him, a not-inconsequential stone nested in his gut, urged him to keep moving.

Hank began dating a woman, Kate, a poet and editor for the local alternative weekly. Just six years his junior, she was nearly age-appropriate. Hank felt stupid for wondering if this heralded some significant maturation within him. They ate in restaurants and visited wine bars and watched mostly good movies in their apartments. They spent a late-spring weekend in Saugatuck, Michigan, with another couple.

As he had with Amanda so long ago, they mocked the corny artsiness of the town while simultaneously allowing themselves to become caught up in the spirit of the place enough to buy three-by-five watercolor paintings of sunsets and other souvenirs they would display with some ill-defined measure of irony. But he could not escape the vague surprise he felt each night, when they lay down in bed—sometimes turning to each other and shedding clothes and sometimes not—that they'd made it another day without his finding some reason to end the whole thing. A matter of time, he thought.

They had just finished lunch at a Cuban restaurant in Logan Square when Hank saw Chase. It was summer again, three years since their evening together. Across the street from where Hank and Kate emerged into the sunlight, Chase sat on the sidewalk, his back curled against the brick wall of a café, a small Tupperware container on the ground between his feet.

"I know that guy," Hank said.

Kate pivoted, looked. "Really? How?"

Hank shook his head, slowly, as if he didn't quite understand the question.

Kate said, "Do you want to say hi?"

Who would mourn Chase's passing when he died? Was there a person out there who would initiate the dance of arrangements for our rituals of grief, who would, through whatever enterprising, track down all the names and numbers of his past associates to collect in honor of his memory? The question was depressingly easy to answer.

Only slightly trickier: would someone be there for Hank when his time came?

He strode across the street, a honking cab swerving to avoid answering the question prematurely.

Though it would have been difficult to imagine it possible those years before, Chase now looked even worse. The rehab, if he'd made it there at all, had not taken. Clearly. Long, greasy hair now framed his gaunt face. An oversized tank top exposed an emaciated chest.

A warm breeze passed, and Hank felt Kate's presence at his side. Hank wondered if he had yet, as Amanda had predicted the last time they spoke, lost the capacity to love another person. Had he passed some point of no return? Or did his rotten little heart still have a few beats left in it?

Chase looked up with those azure eyes. His face was ravaged by years of various abuses, but nothing could change those eyes. "Hank Margolis," he said with a grin, and then pointed a finger to the sky. "Someone's smiling down on us today, motherfucker."

MODERN SOUNDS IN
COUNTRY AND WESTERN

· · · ·

Kat and Smith left Brooklyn on a Tuesday morning in Smith's '05 Ford Ranger pickup, stupidly timing it so they had to endure both bridge and tunnel traffic, as well as a commuter jam through Manhattan and Newark. They wondered—each silently—if they'd made a mistake, if they should just abandon the whole trip, admit defeat in the face of the awful gods of gridlock. By the time they had gotten any distance from their respective neighborhoods (Kat—Flatbush, Smith—Bay Ridge), it was nearly noon. But they continued on and by midafternoon both felt a lifting of pressure from their chests.

They sped across the fields and woods of eastern Pennsylvania, the windows open, stopping to sit in the cab of the truck and eat the lunches they'd packed, looking out at the town of Carlisle, Pennsylvania, home of Dickinson College, which Kat had visited once with her mother a decade before when she was looking at schools. She ended up at Queens College but dropped out after four semesters to spend more time on music. This lunch was spent mostly in silence—they really didn't know each other all that well, and what they did know of one another was mired in the smoky terror of the night they met. Sitting there chewing her cheese sandwich, Kat wondered what might have happened if she'd decided to come to this school. Would she have left halfway through her studies, as she did at Queens? Would she and her sister Beth have started the band they'd spent the past seven years in? And this question, along with nearly every question Kat investigated, led to the inevitable: if she'd chosen Dickinson over Queens, would Beth still be dead?

This had little to do with colleges, of course. Kat could pick almost any event, any moment, any decision of her past, and, in a *Sliding Doors* kind of way that even Kat herself found irritating, it would ultimately come to the question of Beth's life and death. What if Beth had taken up the piano instead of the guitar? What if their mother had been more insistent that they each finish school? What if their father hadn't bailed on them and their mom when they were still kids? All of these butterfly-effect musings fluttered within her mind as she and Smith looked out on the dappled sidewalks below the elms and maples of the campus.

• • • •

Though they assured themselves and each other that they were friends and traveling companions and nothing more, Kat and Smith slept together on the first night of their trip, in a La Quinta Inn outside Roanoke, Virginia. It was inevitable. They'd both wanted to, and they'd both worried about what it would mean. In the moment, what won out was the quiet of being away from the city, the familiar anonymity of the hotel room, and the buzzing pent-up emotions of the past months. There was no stopping it.

After, Smith said, "Well." His hirsute chest still rising and falling with a quick uneven rhythm. The stiff top sheet down across his belly.

"Yeah. Well," Kat said. "Heck of a way to start a road trip."

"I've started them worse."

"Yeah? How?"

Smith rolled to his side to face her.

"One time we got all of our guitars stolen out of the van the night of our first gig," he said. "That was a hell of an omen."

"How was the rest of the tour?"

"Not much better."

He'd been on the road too many times to count, spent too many nights sleeping upright in the seat of a van or in roach-infested motels halfway between nowhere and not-much-better. This was part of the reason he stopped going on the road, why he quit his last band and hadn't joined another, focusing instead on working the soundboard at venues around Brooklyn and Manhattan. He didn't have to lug a soundboard around, and his bed was always just a couple of trains away.

He got up and went to the cooler they'd brought in from the truck, got out a beer. Held it up and Kat nodded. He popped the caps off two IPAs and brought them to the bed. Kat opened Spotify on her phone and put on Tanya Tucker's "It's a Cowboy Lovin' Night," one of her new favorites, then felt sheepish about the choice. But she let it play. More awkward to turn it off now.

"Maybe we should go to Houston, too," Smith said when Tucker sang of the city.

Kat shrugged. "We could. Go see the Old Quarter where Townes played."

"Is it still there?"

"I think so. Beth wanted to check it out when we played there a couple years ago. We didn't, though."

Kat had told her sister it was a waste of time, that she didn't feel like driving around the Houston sprawl in an Uber for two hours looking for a random building where some old cowboy played a show forty years before. Beth relented. Now Kat wonders what they ended up doing that afternoon instead. Probably they got stoned and everybody looked at their phones. Maybe they got tacos.

But now she's considering going hundreds of miles off the proposed path to gaze up at whatever the Old Quarter was now, to maybe sit there in a parking spot listening to Townes Van Zandt play "Pancho and Lefty" and "To Live Is to Fly."

This whole trip was Beth's idea, months before her death. Kat didn't know how serious she'd been about it; maybe it was just some notion that alit momentarily in her mind: a country music pilgrimage. Nashville and Austin and Bakersfield. She'd only mentioned it that once, a weeknight when the two of them were drinking in their apartment, listening to the traffic through the open window. Beth had gotten suddenly and deeply into country. Kat humored her sister's newfound enthusiasm, listened with her to the old records Beth brought home by the armful: Patsy, Willie, Emmylou, Dolly. Being a proper hipster, Kat liked Johnny Cash. She had a harder time with the bands her ears found corny, the Louvin Brothers or Buck Owens and his Buckaroos. Kat assumed it was a semi-ironic thing, like when they would smoke a joint and watch *The Cutting Edge*. She would try to pry her sister away from the stereo, get her across the street to the coffee shop or down the way to the neighborhood bar they liked for some day drinking, but as often as not Beth would say, "Nah, I'm good," and flip to side two of whatever dusty, warped platter she was spinning.

Kat took a pull off her beer and listened to the music, tinny from her phone speaker but echoing deeply in her mind. Smith ran his rough hand along her thigh, wanting more already. Kat turned and kissed him, happy for the distraction.

• • • •

When Beth and Kat and the band left on tour, their second full-length record just released, they were still known only to a few indie-folk enthusiasts. Their first album hadn't been anything like a hit, though it sold well enough that their tiny but respected label didn't drop them, gave them another shot. The second one was a better album all around. Kat's bass playing had improved. She understood better how the sound translated to a recording (before this she really only understood how to play to half-empty bars). Marcellus's drumming was tighter, more restrained—something Beth pushed for. Brad's lead guitar work mingled more fluidly with Beth's rhythm. But it was Beth's voice that had seen the biggest evolution. On the first album, it was good. Better than good. Lovely. But in these sessions it took on deeper tones and satisfyingly ragged edges. She belted out the new tunes she'd penned, with titles like "Georgia O'Keefe" and "Simple Men," songs with a heavier weight of Americana than her previous compositions. As she sang them in the studio, Kat and Marcellus and Brad had to keep from glancing at one another, as if to do so would break whatever spell had come over their leader.

It was near the end of the sessions when she brought in "Yesterday's Tomorrow" and played it for the band on her Martin acoustic. Looking back, Kat wants to remember thinking she couldn't believe her sister had written such a perfect song. It was so simple and familiar, yet so fresh, as if all of humanity had been circling the damn thing for millennia and only Beth was able to reach out, take hold of it, and finally give it shape. "Instant classic," was the tired phrase more than a few reviewers would trot out after hearing it. But tired or not, it made sense. Like "Will You Still Love Me Tomorrow?" or "Save the Last Dance for Me," "Teen Spirit," or "Fade Into You," it was a song that seemed to have existed forever before being plucked from the world's collective consciousness.

But really what Kat had thought in the studio was, *So we're doing a fucking country song?*

The day the band hit the road, the song had yet to hit the airwaves. When it did, though, everything changed. Their shows were suddenly sold out. The band's manager—really an old friend with almost no ex-

157

perience in the music world—was scrambling to move gigs from bars to clubs, and only a week later from those clubs to 2,000-, 2,500-capacity venues. Instead of going directly from Pittsburgh to Chicago, they stopped and did a Tuesday in Cincinnati (sold out). Instead of having a night off after Denver, they did a second show (sold out). The album got a begrudging 9.2 from Pitchfork—though the reviewer seemed to imply that the high score was *despite* "Yesterday's Tomorrow," which they deemed "pleasing but derivative." Beth and Kat had already arranged to do phone interviews with college stations, but were now following those with calls to stations farther right on the dial. They were on the shortlist for the cover of the next issue of *No Depression*. When, in Boise, Marcellus had to get an emergency crown put on a tooth, Kat sat in the waiting room and heard the song emanating from a radio behind the front desk. As ridiculous as it seemed, for Kat it was this—and not any of the other recent and utterly improbable developments—that got her, that told her that their lives were changed. *They're playing us in a dentist's waiting room*, she thought, taking a moment to close her eyes and marvel at the new world her sister had created.

All of this happened while they were away from the one-bedroom-and-a-pullout apartment the sisters shared in Flatbush, while they lugged their gear in a rented trailer off the back of a borrowed van. All of it happened in a matter of five head-spinning weeks. By the time they got back to Brooklyn, the little wrap-up show they'd planned had turned into a three-night sold-out stay at a spot they'd dreamed of playing since they got started.

And wouldn't it have been something had it happened. All those people coming to see a quartet of kids from down the road playing songs they'd recorded only a couple months before—a blip of time. A band at the heart of which were two sisters who, as children, had shared a single set of earbuds in their parents' backseat, listening to

Sleater-Kinney and Le Tigre. Two sisters who learned to harmonize together to an old Wilson Phillips tape Beth found for fifty cents in a pawn shop. Two sisters who came of age getting stoned to Karen O and fucking skinny boys to Feist and imagining their future selves as Björk. Two sisters who'd decided on their respective instruments almost silently, both of them recognizing where the real talent was, one with modest reserve, the other with resignation. Two sisters who'd started a band because why not, who knew, and wouldn't it be fun. Two sisters, two sister, two sisters.

Yes, it would have been something. Some kind of homecoming. Had it not been for the four explosives planted by a homegrown terrorist cell, explosives that killed thirty-two concertgoers and three of the four members of the band on stage.

• • • •

The middle of the country opened up with a flash. It was somehow nothing that Kat had ever seen. She'd traveled coast to coast before, of course, but here in the cab of Smith's truck the land looked both comforting and terrifyingly large. She scooted lower in the passenger seat, put her knees up on the glove compartment. A semi burst past them on the left and made Kat's heart lurch and her palms sweat.

"Do you have nightmares?" she asked Smith.

"About the thing?"

"Yeah."

"I have," Smith said. "I wouldn't say I *do*. It's not a regular thing. Do you?"

"Yeah."

"A lot?"

"Enough."

Smith said, "For me it's like I get zoned out. I'm not thinking about it exactly. I'm not really thinking about anything. I was never like that before."

"Maybe you're checking out," Kat said. "Like a defense mechanism. To avoid your brain reliving it."

"Maybe."

Smith had been there running the soundboard. He and Kat first spoke that afternoon at the sound check, and then later in the green room when he came in to make sure everyone felt good about their levels. He asked if they would be opening with "Yesterday's Tomorrow." Beth told him they were still working on the set list, and Brad the guitarist mumbled, "That's the one everybody wants to hear" with a sort of pouty shrug, like he was being put upon.

Smith said, in the lightest tone he could muster, "Hey, worse problems to have," and Brad gave him a sideways glare. What Smith wanted to say to him was *Do you know how many bands send demos here every day, you little dickhead? How many kids are out there playing to a dozen people or less in crappy dives, standing up on eight-inch stages dreaming of the moment you all are living right now?*

There was nothing odd about the night, except maybe a little more excitement in the air. This was a little band from the neighborhood who'd had a breakout hit. That doesn't happen all the time. So, as Smith noted to a friend before the show started, everyone was feeling very *Rocky II*.

They took the stage right at nine o'clock, after two by-the-numbers indie-folk openers who Smith guessed would never play a crowd this big again. Beth had a warm smile for the crowd. She was a good face for a band. A pretty face, for sure, but what Smith noticed was that she knew how to give to a crowd, how to make them feel like the night was about them. She stepped to the mic and said, "Well, hi there, Brooklyn," and laughed when her fans went crazy. She said, "We're gonna play you some songs, if you don't mind."

The band played a couple lesser known tunes—lesser known to Smith, anyway—and then started "Yesterday's Tomorrow," the audience screaming with delight. As they got into the second verse, the place turned into something else. Like chemistry. A thing goes from one state of matter to another. But instead of liquid to gas, this was a concert turned to smoke and dust and terror. The first explosion happened somewhere between the bar and the board, where Smith sat. He didn't know if the walls of the sound booth protected him, but by the time the second bomb went off, an interminable half-second later, he was on the floor, those booth walls collapsed on top of him, and though he got his head knocked around as people ran over him and fell on top of him, he was still all too aware of the screams. He could still taste the dust and smoke. He could still understand when the third and fourth bombs exploded, though he would find out only later that it was likely that second one that killed the band.

He has no memory of being transported to the hospital. He has no memory of a moment when he understood that the violence was over. His roommate Geoff and Geoff's girlfriend came to see him, and it was only through them that he started to get a handle on what had happened, that it was not some poorly installed gas line. Not an accident. That it was an attack. That night Smith got a Facebook message from his dad in Minneapolis. *You ok?* it read. And when Smith said he was, his dad wrote back, *Ok good I'm glad yr not dead.* Smith started to write *Me too* but then erased it and figured they'd both said enough.

• • • •

They slept late into the morning. Smith went to a diner and brought back eggs and hash browns and limp buttered toast. They ate and then fucked in the shower and got back on the road. On a Knoxville radio station they heard a commercial for a workout DVD called "Cowboy

Sweat," which made line dancing to pop country into a fat-burning regimen. Snippets of songs from Toby and Garth and Reba played as a woman with a proud southern accent shouted about how it was time to kick up their boots and lose those saddlebags.

"Yeehaw," Smith said.

When they stopped for lunch Smith logged into his Airbnb account, searched Nashville, and found a tent in some dude's backyard on the east side.

"A tent?" Kat said.

"Look at this," he said, turning his phone's screen to her. It was a tent, but looked as big as a room, with a queen-sized bed and mosquito netting. "It's like *Out of Africa* or something."

When they got there it was better and stranger than they'd expected. A wooden floor was covered with overlapping rugs, and wool blankets were tossed over worn leather chairs.

"Colonialism chic," Kat said.

It was seven o'clock already, so Kat suggested they just stay in for the night. There was a crappy old Crosley record player and a handful of LPs. They stretched out on the bed, getting drunk on red wine and listening to a worn copy of *Nashville Skyline*, Kat playing "Girl from the North Country" again and again, marveling at the way Dylan's bizarre Jim Nabors voice played improbably and beautifully off of Johnny's unadorned baritone.

The next day Smith fetched them some barbecue and a copy of *Nashville Scene*. Flipping pages, he read aloud their options for places to visit and shows to see.

"There's the Hall of Fame, of course. That's something we should probably do, right? And that South Broadway stuff?"

"Isn't that, like, all tourist shit?" Kat said.

"Well, what are we?"

Kat said nothing to that, and nothing to Smith's suggestion of Ryman Auditorium, where the Opry had started back in the day, and nothing to the Bluebird Cafe and to the list of shows in various venues around town. It took Smith an embarrassing length of time to understand that something was wrong. He watched her absently drum her pulled pork sandwich with a pickle, and only then did it dawn on him that in the past two days Kat had not ventured beyond the truck and their accommodations. She hadn't come into a restaurant or gas station. And was it possible that even back in Brooklyn they'd only seen each other in her apartment? He could not think of a time they'd gotten coffee or a beer, could not recall a stroll through the neighborhood.

"We don't have to do anything," he said. "But we did come all this way."

"Yeah," she said quietly.

"Nothing bad is going to happen."

She finally met his eyes. "You don't know that."

• • • •

She tried not to show any evidence of the panic rising in her as they entered the Country Music Hall of Fame. In the lobby, hundreds of people milled about, drinking bottles of beer and chatting. She wiped her palms on her jeans as they strode through the exhibits, gazing at the instruments, the elaborate dresses and embroidered Nudie suits hung on headless mannequins. Smith put his arm around her waist as they watched a video of Wanda Jackson belting out "Hard Headed Woman." She leaned into him.

"I need a drink," she said.

A few blocks away, at Robert's Western World, they watched a six-piece run through a set of crowd-pleasers. It was only three in the afternoon, but the bar and all of Broadway Street were loaded with people well on their way to drunk. A few were already there. The band was tight, though the overeager drummer seemed like he'd prefer to be playing Zeppelin over George Jones, adding a few too many fills to his shuffle. But she liked that he was there anyway. She and Smith both knew that a gig was a gig, and she figured the drummer knew that too.

"Do you miss playing?" she asked Smith.

When he was honest with himself, Smith would admit that he never knew what music he should be playing. He'd started in high school, playing hardcore in friends' parents' basements around the suburbs of Minneapolis. Then, after a ten-month stint in a jazzy post-rock Chicago quintet, he made it to New York, where he played rhythm guitar in a mellow, pop-minded indie outfit. None of these felt quite right. None of them seemed like *his* music. He'd tried his hand at songwriting himself, but they never came out any good and he didn't enjoy the act anyway. But he loved music. He loved hearing it, any genre, any style. Even the sloppiest hardcore he'd played as a teen seemed to him like the highest calling a human could ask for. Music was the most accurate, most immediate, most articulate expression of humanness he could imagine. And yet, for him, playing always left him feeling slightly empty. It wasn't that he lacked ability. On the contrary, he was a perfectly capable player, and he'd never been booted from any group he'd ever been in. He was always the one to leave. It was as if it was only a matter of time before the novelty of a new group wore off and all he could see, all he could *hear*, was the windy gap between what he'd always thought he'd wanted and the reality of what he was doing.

"Not really," he said. But this wasn't exactly true. There was something he missed, and it was the feeling of possibility that this next group, this next show, this next song, this next chord could achieve what he'd always thought music should: a brief moment of bond between himself and the rest of the world, even if that bond was unlikely.

He supposed this was what he loved about Beth's voice. It seemed clear that she'd made that bond happen. Smith didn't tell Kat, but after the attack he'd bought their record and listened to it near-constantly for months. In fact, he couldn't recall listening to anything else in that time before Kat reached out to him, and that was why it had felt like such a miracle, or a terrible prank, when she did. The record, and "Yesterday's Tomorrow" in particular, did a strange thing to him; instead of forcing him to relive that terrible night, it allowed him to live it completely, as it should have been: full of drinks and music and all of the potential that music, at its best, makes real.

"Do you miss it?" he asked Kat.

"I miss the attention," she said. "I know that sounds terrible, but I do."

"It doesn't sound terrible."

"Maybe it would have changed after a while. You know, people say fame is this awful thing when you're actually in it. But, like, it had just started for us. It *just* happened, and then . . ."

The band on stage broke into "White Lightning."

Smith said, "I guess the question to ask at some point is what you do now. You going to keep playing?"

Kat watched the people below and thought about the concert in Las Vegas where that piece of shit sat in a hotel room above and picked people off with a semi-automatic. She thought of the show in Paris, the nightclub in Orlando. She thought of the school shootings, too many to recall. All those poor children. She watched the people laugh and do their best to two-step, and she thought of the people who came out to see the band that night, the ones who never went home. She thought of Brad and Marcellus, and as her mind landed upon her sister, a voice sounded behind her.

"Hey, you two, can I give you these?"

It was a young woman, blond and lean and muscular, with a bright, too-perfect smile behind frosted pink lips. She was holding two sheets of paper out. Kat and Smith took them. The young woman said, "You never had so much fun getting ripped, y'all," and turned away. The sheets were flyers for *Cowboy Sweat*, the instructional fitness program they'd heard a commercial for on the radio the day before. At the bottom it read "Honkytonk your butts off!!!" There was a picture of a crowd of white people in pearl-buttoned shirts kicking up their boots, having the time of their lives.

· · · ·

When Kat woke up in the hospital the day after the attack, her mom was there in the room. It would have been disorienting enough just coming to, but of course they also had her on painkillers for her fractured femur and shattered wrist. On top of all that, she had a pretty severe concussion. So she didn't quite understand where she was. When her mom said, "Do you remember what happened?" Kat's mind sped past the attack, the explosions, the screams and the pain and the fear—all of which would flood her soon enough—and landed on a moment right before the show.

"We got into a fight," she said.

"What?" her mom said. "Who?"

"Me and Beth."

Her mother's face trembled, and she placed a hand over her mouth. This would be what Kat would come back to, the moment she would remember, the moment she knew, not yet in her brain but somewhere else, past that, somewhere in her gut, her heart, her soul, that her sister was dead.

Her mother told her that a group had claimed responsibility, a far right wing Christian extremist group. Some speculated that the attack was specific to the band—some overly ambitious theories about the "liberal gentrification of country music." But it soon became clear that it had been far more random. They targeted Brooklyn, yes, but the venue and band playing mattered little. It was a sold-out show. That was the main thing. They wanted to kill a lot of people. Kat's mother told her that the president had tweeted something noncommittal about it. She couldn't seem to care. She knew she should. She should be filled with rage and that rage should be directed at the people who planned and carried out the attack. But she couldn't. The grief had taken over, and there was no room for anything else except the recurring thought that it seemed impossible that no one had ever invented a time machine.

Kat got in touch with Smith six months later. She'd seen YouTube clips of him once or twice, being interviewed about that night. She liked the way he listened to the interviewer's questions, as if he hadn't heard them before, as if all the questions didn't come down to just one: what was it like? She had turned down countless requests from local tv stations to the *Today Show* to the *New Yorker*. She couldn't see the point, and she couldn't see their questions as anything but morbid curiosity. But when she watched Smith talking into a mic, she saw a generosity of spirit at work, and she liked that his appearances on her laptop screen challenged her to be kinder.

She reached out to him via Facebook, sent a message asking if he'd like to meet up. She couldn't quite articulate why she wanted to talk to him. She couldn't even think of what she might have to say. But she asked nonetheless, intuiting that they might have something to give one another. Smith replied that yes, he would like to meet, and they made a plan for that Saturday afternoon.

She didn't feel completely comfortable inviting him to her place, but she had all but stopped going out by then, having groceries delivered, spending most of her days and nights going through Beth's records, flipping them over and dropping the needle and obsessively googling country music stars of yesteryear. She only barely remembered Smith from before the show—at that point she'd been pretty much on autopilot through sound checks. But when he came through her door she recalled him stopping by the green room to make sure they were all satisfied with the sound. She'd met a lot of sound guys, and most of them tended to be dicks. She remembered feeling grateful that their tour was ending with a nice one.

Bearded in a flannel shirt and rolled Levi's, he might have been any dude walking around Brooklyn. But he wasn't. She understood that no one was special except to those for whom they were. This man was special only because she decided he was.

She got them beers and sat on the floor across the coffee table from him. Spring was in bloom outside the open window.

"I'm sorry about your sister," Smith said. "She had a fuckin' hell of a voice."

After that every few days Smith would take the R train to the Q to Kat's place, where they would drink and listen to Beth's records. Like Kat, Smith had never known much about country music beyond the usual things one picked up along the way: a couple Hank Williams tunes he could hum, that "Okie from Muskogee" song, some of the unavoidable '90s pop garbage. But the two of them, without saying much about it, seemed to take on these records as one might a puzzle that needed to be solved. Like something from a movie—two unsuspecting people thrown into a scenario where they had to put together the clues in order to find . . . what, exactly? They didn't know. So maybe it was less a puzzle and more a compulsion, an urge radiating out from somewhere deep within them, a shifting epicenter they couldn't quite pinpoint. The afternoon sun would slip and a bruise-like dusk would come over the city and Kat and Smith would flip from A-sides to B-sides and talk little save for the tidbits of arcana gleaned from back cover notes.

After two months of this, she asked if he might be up for a little drive.

· · · ·

In Texarkana they checked into a Hampton Inn and took each other's clothes off. Kat wanted to drive the next morning, and they set off for Austin, both of them forgetting completely that they'd talked about swinging down to Houston.

They made Austin in six hours, taking in the Texas landscape around them, so flat and arid, so intensely hot, so immense it didn't take too much imagination to think it might go on forever. They listened to Willie Nelson and Jimmie Dale Gilmore and Lucinda Williams. Such a feeling of freedom swelled in Kat that she didn't want to arrive, but once they did and were checked into a room at the hotel on South Congress, she felt strangely at home. She told Smith this and he said, "Yeah, Austin's like a hug."

Kat decided to get herself a pair of boots. Inside a shop down the street, she said she wanted to buy Smith a pair, too. She picked up a pair of Lucchese boots that cost eleven hundred dollars. "Try these ones," she said.

"That's way too much money," he protested.

"I have too much money," she said. It was true. "Yesterday's Tomorrow" had filled her bank account to overflowing, and she found herself instinctually wanting it gone.

She paid and he put them on. "These are officially the second most valuable thing I own after my truck," Smith said.

Outside, they looked down at the boots on their feet and laughed as they walked to a food truck, where Smith insisted on paying. A woman nearby did a magnificent rendition of "Coat of Many Colors" on a cheap Fender acoustic. Kat dropped a twenty in her case.

The sun began to fall, and Kat and Smith followed a small stream of people to the river. "It's the bats," Smith said. They sat on the grass and smelled the nearly overwhelming stench of guano. Soon, the bats began to emerge from under the bridge. A few at first, then more and more, the whole colony of millions streaming out, silhouetted against the fading light. People applauded. Children pointed and ran, flapping their arms.

Kat leaned against Smith, and after a few minutes of silence, Smith said, "My dad messaged me after that night to see if I was still alive. I told him I was but haven't heard from him since."

"Is your mom around?"

"She died when I was fourteen."

"Jesus."

"Yeah." He scratched at his beard. "When you got in touch with me, it was like a miracle. It was like you saved my life. I don't have anyone. And I don't want you to hear that and think I'm asking you to fix that. I'm not. I'm just telling you."

"Ok," Kat said gently. "Thank you for telling me." She set her head on his shoulder.

Walking back toward the hotel, she said, "Can I tell you something now?" He looked down at her. "And you have to promise not to tell anyone."

"I promise."

Kat breathed deeply. "Right before the show that night, Beth and I got into a fight."

"What about?"

"She was going to break up the band."

"She told you that?"

Kat nodded. "She was acting kind of weird and I was giving her a hard time, being all 'Cheer up!' and 'What's wrong with you?' This was our big night, right? She said 'Nothing,' but I knew something was up and then it got kind of tense and I asked her what was up again and again, and now I wish I had just left her alone because I wish I didn't know. She was dumping us. She had a whole plan to go solo. She said she still wanted me to play bass with her *sometimes*, but I knew that was just a bone she was throwing me. And I was embarrassed that I'd been going around thinking we were one thing, and all that time she saw me and the guys as dead weight. I was so mad at her. I've never been that mad at her in my life. I called her a selfish bitch and a sell-out and a wannabe. I called her Taylor Swift. Five minutes later we were out on stage, and ten minutes after that she was dead. And all I can think is why the fuck did she tell me. Why couldn't she have just walked away. Because I want to miss her purely and I can't."

Smith said nothing, which was exactly what Kat wanted. They walked along, both of them suddenly exhausted, past the restaurants and bars and cafes, back to their hotel room, where they fell asleep with their boots on.

· · · ·

The next morning Kat awoke to the smell of coffee and found Smith in his boxers sitting on the windowsill drinking from a steaming cup. "Right there," he said, pointing to another coffee on the side table. She went to the bathroom and showered, and when she came back, Smith was looking out at the street below. He said, "Some kind of festival thing they're setting up out here."

Kat went to the window. Their stretch of South Congress was closed off, and a stage had been erected at the end of the block. She sat on the bed and drank her coffee.

Smith continued to watch the people below. He wondered if they had a good soundman. He wondered if they *needed* a good soundman. He wondered how much it would cost to live here, to pack up and move. He didn't have much money, but he also didn't have many possessions, and surely he could find a gig or two in the self-proclaimed music capital of the world. Maybe he'd try his hand at producing, find some kids with a bit of talent and make a go of it. He wondered if Kat would move with him, if maybe she was thinking something similar.

A group of people approached the stage and unrolled a vinyl banner across the front. It took him a moment to make out the words, but when he did he nearly choked on his coffee.

"You're not going to believe what this is down there," he said.

"What?"

"This is too good."

"What *is* it?" Kat said, getting up and coming to him.

He looked at her with wide, beaming eyes. "It's *Cowboy Sweat.*"

• • • •

They came to understand that it was a free, live demonstration of the workout. A trio of women in spandex and pink cowgirl hats seemed to be running the setup, standing on stage and pointing people in every direction. Each of the spandex women took a turn testing her headset mic. Dozens of people—singles, couples, whole families—started showing up, lining up parallel to the stage.

"We have to," Smith said.

"Not a chance."

"It's not even a debate," Smith said, pulling on a t-shirt with a picture of an accordion on it and the words *This is my polka face.* "We're putting on those fancy boots," he said, "and we are going to honkytonk our butts off."

By the time they got down to the street, the demonstration was starting. The three women strutted on stage while toned men and women in *Cowboy Sweat* shirts arranged people into lines.

"All right, y'all," one of the spandex women said. "Are you ready to shake what your mamas gave you?"

Another said, "Are you ready to kick up those heels and tone up those buns?"

The third said, "Y'all are about to work up a cowboy sweat!"

Along with a person assigned to each line, the women led the crowd through the steps of a dance called the *hoedown showdown* before "Boot Scootin' Boogie" boomed from the speakers. Over the song, the women yelled words of encouragement: "That's it, y'all!" and "Keep going, y'all!" and sometimes, getting straight to the point, just an ebullient "*Y'all!*"

Kat stumbled trying to keep the steps straight, but Smith seemed to get it right away. He shuffled and spun right along with the line leaders.

"Why are you good at this?" Kat shouted.

"Boot Scootin' Boogie" went straight into "Achy Breaky Heart," and the crowd let out a cry of approval. Kat rolled her eyes, but Smith sang along with exaggerated fervor and kept up his confusingly competent dancing. She wondered if he was doing this for her, playing the goofball role to make her laugh, to make her happy. Purposeful or not, it was working, and she appreciated it.

After twenty minutes of kicks and spins and shimmies under the big old Texas sun, Kat's shirt was sweat-logged. Beads hung on Smith's brow. She wondered if her face was as red as his. The music faded and one of the women said, "All right, all right. Can you feel that burn?" The crowd whooped. "I tell you what," she went on, "we're gonna take it down a notch or two for just a minute to catch our breath. Now this is a simple little step . . ." She showed them the move, an easy shuffle-spin-dip combo. Smith watched and mimicked.

Kat said to him, "You're ridiculous."

"You're jealous."

Smith's antics had nearly caused Kat to forget the pain she carried in her chest, the pain that radiated out, spread through her like an infection. She'd almost lost track of the grief that swirled around her like whirlwind. And she might have been free of that pain and that grief for another minute, another ten, fifteen minutes—that seemed to be the limit—had it not been for the first strum of her sister's Martin acoustic guitar sailing out of the speakers. For a half-second Kat thought that she must be mistaken, a trick of her mind, a product of the limited number of notes and chords available to a composer of tunes, but the entrance of her own bass confirmed it, and a tremor took over her heart. Smith heard it, too. He watched her, waiting for a signal of what might happen next, of what to do.

The people around them started their twists and dips. And then Beth's voice rang out. Kat's legs went weak and she crouched to the pavement, balled herself up, hands laced over the back of her head. Smith went down, too, put his hands on her shoulders, leaning over her, as if protecting her from something physical, something deadly raining down on them. For the first time, she recalled the moment of the initial explosion. They'd gotten through two songs and started on the third, the one everybody wanted. The cheers of the crowd returned to her ears. Beth's voice was numinous, but then it always had been. Now, as that voice sang out over the dancing crowd, over the whole city it seemed, Kat understood that Beth was right to leave her and Brad and Marcellus behind. They wouldn't have been able to keep up with her. Worse, she would have had to limit herself to keep the gap between them from becoming too obvious. They were a fine band, but only fine. They were Big Brother and the Holding Company. They were The Sugarcubes. They were the other two in Destiny's Child. Talented musicians, occasionally brilliant, but dim lights in comparison to the fiery star in their midst.

Kat watched the synchronized movements of the legs all around her and listened to the song as if hearing it for the first time.

. . . .

Kat and Smith continued west but didn't make it to Bakersfield. Austin had taken it out of them. Their last full stop was at the Joshua Tree Inn, the dusty desert oasis where Gram Parsons died. In 1973, Parsons—the country singer who built a hippie lifestyle atop a southern gentleman's upbringing—OD'd, as many who knew him had predicted he would. The story most people know, though, is what happened next, when his longtime friend, fueled by booze and bad judgment, heisted Parsons' casket and drove it back to Joshua Tree and set it on fire—a makeshift cremation and an infantile way for anyone's tenure on this earth to end.

Kat had known the story, but never listened to the man's music until after the attack, when she found his records in Beth's collection. What a shame, she thought, that this foolish and gentle soul, this fragile voice, should be so eclipsed by his death. She mourned the fact that Beth, too, would come to be known more for her death than her music. She would be the one with that great voice, that song—the one that died in an attack on their concert. Remember? It was on the news.

Outside room number eight in that dingy one-story motel, pilgrims left tokens of their appreciation for the spirit of Gram: cigarettes and records, flowers and bottles of booze. Smith set a beer down, adding to the collection. Kat went to her bag and fished out a guitar pick, leaned over and balanced it on top of Smith's beer.

Neither Kat nor Smith knew what would become of them once they returned home to Brooklyn. They sat in chairs by the motel pool and popped bottles. Smith pulled the boots from his feet and set them on the concrete, said, "Yes, ma'am, these are some boots."

There seemed to be no one else staying at the motel that night. They were alone, surrounded only by the vast, silent desert. After a moment, Kat felt a quick and terrible panic in her chest, as if suddenly remem-

175

bering something crucial. She bolted upright in her lounger, looked around at the low hills, barely visible in the post-dusk darkness. They'd been traveling for more than a week now, days upon days spent tracing fingers along maps and phone screens, looking at where they'd been and where they were headed, but now, in the vast desert, she couldn't tell which direction was which.

Smith saw her chest rising and falling, and then her eyes found his. He watched her and she watched him watching. She studied the shadows cast across the topography of his face and then said, "Bakersfield will still be there."

She sat back and they drank and on the other side of the motel a semitruck blew through the small pool of the motel's lights.

GLOSSARY FOR
THE END OF DAYS

· · · ·

A.

Abbeville, Iowa. Town where the farm was, with the barn and the goats
and the one cow, who was so old and sagged you could see the peaks
of her back ridge pointing up through her hide and who hadn't pro-
duced a drop of milk in probably a decade. There were chickens, too,
and about a thousand cats either stalking the mice or sleeping in piles
under shafts of sun. It wasn't a bad spread, all in all, if you just looked
from the outside and ignored all the boney girls dragging ass through
the garden and sloshing pails of water to the bath out back or the dudes
trying to figure out how to chop firewood, nearly taking their own legs
out. The people of Abbeville pretty much ignored us, figuring we were
just a bunch of hippies, which I guess a lot of us were. Abbeville isn't
too far from where Edgar and I grew up, or too different. No one's ever
heard of Abbeville—or they hadn't, anyway, before we came along.

B.

Barrett. He was the leader. I always assumed it was his farm, but later
during the investigation and what all, it came out that it actually be-
longed to another member, this woman Leah. She slept in the shared

room—which was actually three rooms with the walls between bashed down—with all the rest of us, while Barrett had the only private bedroom, so I guess that's why I assumed. Barrett was older than anyone there (except Leah, who was probably past sixty). He was in his forties, probably mid-forties, and he had shiny black hair like a Labrador. When I first got there, my first day even visiting, Barrett sat me down outside. It was spring, the kind of day where you're just more open to anything because it's so goddamn beautiful outside with the sun and the clouds and the little wind gusts and you think anything is possible on a day like this. On a day like this, your life could change. So Barrett, he sits me down on this metal chair out by the garden and he pulls his own metal chair right there in front of me and we just look at each other for a good minute. More. And normally I'd think what's this guy's story, but there was something about him, Barrett. Trustworthy. Finally he says, You have questions.

C.

Catechism. What we said each morning before breakfast. It didn't have anything to do with Catholics, which I guess is what most people think of when they hear this part. I wouldn't even know about that. Growing up, Dad's religion was getting fucked up and chasing worn-out tail down at Sully's, and Mom's was whatever real murder show was on the tube. But at Ninth Day we went through the Q&A so often I was doing it in my sleep. Literally. I dreamed it. I can't say I really believed it at the beginning, but I sure as shit said it. *How do we come to know the Vision?* We know the Vision when we know ourselves. *How do we come to know ourselves?* We know ourselves when we shed our desires for material comfort. *Where does the Vision reside?* The Vision resides in the souls of the family. *Who is in the family?* All who believe and have the courage to live the belief. *When will we meet the Vision?* On the day of the final ascension.

D.

Discretion. The word Barrett used. We were sent out to spread the message of Ninth Day, but told not to let on too much about the specifics of the graduation system. Or about life at the farm. In surrounding towns we'd swing into coffee shops and lunch counters and other places of leisure and casually chat with the locals. We had pamphlets, of course. Everyone's got pamphlets. But, Barrett warned me my first time out, don't whip those out willy-nilly. And he didn't give me a script. Said people could smell that a mile away. He told me to be honest. Well, honest within reason. He said, There are people who won't understand, and the truth we have here can be a little shocking. How would you feel if you were trying to enjoy your meatloaf sandwich and all of a sudden some kid you've never seen before, some kid looks like he's been out rolling in the dirt and smells like sour goat's milk, comes along telling you about the Vision? You'd feel like getting the hell out of there. Calling somebody.

So we used discretion. Only talk about Ninth Day to the most open. Only break out the pamphlets to the most welcoming of the most open. We had a few visitors in those months before the end, but those were always people someone already knew, some old friend, some lost soul from way back. Or the occasional guy coming around and playing like he was interested because he was trying to lay one of our women. We never got anyone cold. But still we went out, chatted, and passed along pamphlets to the kindest and most patient, usually young ones like us, or motherly types who looked at us like it was somehow their fault we had grime blooming on our skin. Some folks want to feel responsible for the whole world.

E.

Edgar, he's the one who got into Ninth Day first. I thought he was putting me on. Not because it sounded loopy as all hell, which of course it did to my ears back then, but more because I'd never known Edgar to take anything seriously. Back home we used to drive up and down Lincoln Highway—well, our little strip of it, anyway—where it goes through downtown, such as it is, and park our cars, my Galaxie or his El Camino, at McDonald's on one end and the SudsyWash on the other, sucking down Cokes spiked with whatever we could afford and shooting the shit about his rebuilt tranny or those nimrods with the ground effects under their Toyotas or whatever girl we were trying to charm before heading over to get blotto in that dark corner of Sully's where the Corona neon went out forever ago. Anyway, we were both working security at the library in those days, keeping the college kids from stealing those big expensive art books or giving each other tugs in their own dark corners. It was the first of May, I remember, because this undergraduate girl, real cutie, kept telling everyone who came to the desk, Happy May Day, and I kept saying, Mayday! Mayday! We're going down! And Edgar, he comes to where I've got my feet up on the desk where the circulation kids sort the returns, maybe twenty minutes from knocking off, and he's shaking his head like he just saw something ridiculous, like unspeakably ridiculous, and then he says to me—serious as hell, this fucking guy—he says, I found the path, Abe.

F.

Food. You'd have thought that with all the gardening we did, all the milking of those goats and slaughtering of chickens (the worst thing I'd ever seen in my life up until that point, all those headless fuckers running around like drunks before dropping and bleeding out into the dust), we would have had some decent grub on the table. But no. Every morning we ate millet. Not oatmeal, not cornflakes. No eggs. Just goddamn millet with goat's milk. Lunch and dinner were creamed chicken with plain rice, barely seasoned and half-warm. A paranoid person would have suspected Barrett of hoarding chocolates and what all up in his room, but I don't think so. In those first days I would choke down the chicken mush and catch Barrett watching me with this look that reminded me it was all a test, a small sacrifice. And who was I to bitch about it? No one questioned Barrett. It was a given that he knew what was best for us. A natural fact. Like gravity. I'm going to question gravity? Pointless.

G.

Guilt. That's what they say I'm suffering: a type of survivor's guilt. Like it's so simple. Like I'm some line in a big shrink's book. Moving on.

H.

Heron. It came and stayed all that summer. Perched up in an elm next to the barn, then, at dusk, swooped down smooth as you can imagine to the ground and danced through the blue light, stabbing its beak at the ground. I'd sit cross-legged in the weedy grass and watch him, hoping he'd get just a little closer. Others would come out and watch for a minute, then wander back to the house for evening sharing group. I'd stay until it was dark, until I couldn't see him anymore. The only other person who ever gave the impression she gave a shit about the bird was Candy. None of the girls really talked to me, which was strange since I'd always done all right with the ones back home. I mean, we were all celibate at Ninth Day anyway, but a little flirting wouldn't have kept us from advancing toward the Vision, right? Little joking around? Little touch on the arm after catechism and before millet? But once, just once, Candy sat there in the field with me and the heron while the light faded. It was sort of like intimacy.

If I could have saved any one of them, aside from Edgar, it would have been Candy.

I.

I. As in, me. What do you want to know? I'm twenty-five as of last month. I have three tattoos, all of which are visible if I take my shirt off. I have a brother, Mike, who I haven't talked to in three years and another who got hit by a train and killed when he was seventeen. I was twelve then, I guess. His name was Chris, but everyone called him Carlos because for some reason he had kind of darkish skin and black hair, where the rest of us—Mom, Dad, Mike, and me—we all look like we could be in those commercials for Norwegian cruises. I mean, except for our fucked-up teeth and hacking smoker's coughs and basic malnourishment. We're really pale, is what I'm saying. I don't know who started calling him Carlos. One of his friends, I guess. Maybe Stenny or Todd or some other dipshit blowing his cash every night down at Sully's these days. Whoever it was, even Mom ended up calling him Carlos after a while, after he took a shine to the new name and wouldn't answer to anything else. Shit, I'm surprised they didn't put it on his gravestone. I thought they should have, like in quotes, thought he would have wanted it like that. I never said anything, though. Even at twelve I knew enough not to start making weird suggestions to people who just lost their kid.

I also used to be an excellent skateboarder and chess player. Moving on.

J.

Jenny. Miss Jenny, we call her. Sometimes we call her other things, but always nice things. Well, not nice like we'd say it in front of her. But you know, complimentary. Guys being guys and showing off. That kind of shit. Stupid shit. Anyway, she's the one who suggested I write all this down when I was having trouble expressing myself in group, and when I couldn't write it down because there was too much to say and where do I start and all, she told me to do it this way, alphabetical. Simplify it, she was like. Slow down. So I'm doing it this way.

And really I'm just writing it for Miss Jenny since she's the only person who's going to see it. Though of course she'll say I'm writing it for myself, but you know what I mean, Miss J.

K.

Knot. I read a book (not a lot else to do here) about a group of people moving out to the country to live off the land and the guy who wrote the book called them a knot of dreamers and I really liked that. Made sense to me. Because that's how it felt right at the peak of Ninth Day, late August, working through that heat and sleeping hard each night and sitting together through prayer with all that corn growing up tall as any of us in the fields all around the farm.

The others didn't believe me. Didn't believe I believed. I'm a smart-ass person and I know sometimes it seems like I don't take anything seriously, and maybe most of the time that's true, but for all the jokes I made about not knowing Paradise would smell so much like cow shit or when do I get my seventy-two virgins, by that point in late August I really did believe. Like I've never believed anything else in my life. And it wasn't brainwashing any more than your more popular religions are. Christianity and Judaism and Islam and what all. I knew the Vision would become manifest. I fucking knew it like you know a dog barks and a baby cries for its mom. Natural fact. And whether my brothers and sisters trusted it or not, I saw them just that way. We were a new kind of family, all twisted up together in this great, beautiful knot.

L.

Library. This is where, if I'd had half a brain, I would have sensed something was up. Barrett sent me back to that library where Edgar and I used to work to pick up some books he'd ordered. I jumped at the chance, since we weren't allowed to bring our cars to the farm and so I hadn't driven in months. Barrett has this great Ford pickup from the early '70s. Powder blue. Four on the floor. Cherry condition. I'd been eyeing it for a while, but the only person besides Barrett I'd ever seen driving it was Edgar, who got sent on errands to the grocery and wherever else every once in a while. So when Barrett tossed me the keys I figured, man, I'd done something right. And then, at the front door, everyone else back at the dining room table finishing up their millet, Barrett slipped two dollars into my hand, sneaky-like, and said, There's that ice cream shop down from the library. You know it, right? He shrugged. He was all, Every once in a while a man needs to treat himself. I'm telling you I thought right there that I was his new right-hand man, his new go-to. He could see past my humor and defense mechanisms (as you call them, Miss J.) to what was really in me.

I drove those roads, flanked on either side by corn, the truck rumbling under me, feeling like I'd maybe never felt before. Worth a goddamn. The books Barrett had sent me for were a few about gardening and some special version of the Bible and a copy of the Koran and one about medicinal herbs and plants. I remember that they were month-long check-outs and the stamp on the receipt said September 23. I remember because that's my birthday. I set the stack in the cab of the truck, which was angled at the curb out front, and then wandered into the ice cream place feeling overwhelmed by the choices and lights and colors. I got a scoop of peanut butter and chocolate in a waffle cone and ate that fucker slow as I could sitting there in the cab of that cherry Ford. It was like I was back cruising the strip with Edgar. Or it was like being a kid. Or both. But better.

M.

Marc and Melody. But also Will and Erin and Jane and Davis and Gemma and Leah and Sanjoy and Amy and Elliot and Horner and Sunshine and Howie and Becky and Candy and Edgar.

N.

Ninth Day. Barrett said that all the world's religions were a little right and a little wrong. He said that all of these groups and doctrines came out of a gut understanding of the divine. He said that we all have the knowledge of God inside us, but it's really hard to get to, and so you have all these groups and their leaders picking up on just a little bit here and a little bit there. Then they filled in all the gaps with whatever made sense in their time and their place. So the founders of Ninth Day brought all the religions' ideas together, mapped their overlaps and their contradictions, separated out the literal from the just-story parts, and found the true way. According to Barrett there were other Ninth Day groups all over the world, but I never saw any proof of this—not that I asked for any. Barrett said there were others, so there were others. It wasn't until the investigation that I heard we were the only ones. I don't know if that makes any difference.

O.

Optimal recruit. That's what I was, according to the people on my case. An optimal recruit for cults and other nefarious organizations. Young. White. Poor. Uneducated. Disconnected from family. Spiritually unmoored. Well, sure, when you put it that way. Everyone was all, Mmhmm, that's the profile. Looking at me like they were so not surprised. Even though I wasn't that young or poor or uneducated. I went to high school, for chrissake. Can't argue with spiritually unmoored, though. Not the family thing neither.

P.

Paramedics. They had to bring them in from two other towns, and still it took most of the afternoon.

Q.

Quiet. Like, in the evenings after we were done with work and prayer. That's all I can think of for Q. Moving on.

R.

Rapture. Not that Barrett ever used the word, and we didn't tick the days off some old-ass calendar or anything like that, but I think we all knew on some level that was the endgame. Moving out of this world and to the Vision. I mean, it was in the catechism: the day of the final ascension. End of the world. What else.

S.

September 21. Two days before my birthday. Barrett sent me out again to pick up books from the library. This time he handed me a twenty. Go have a couple beers, he said. Good old joint called Sully's. Martha behind the bar, pretty lady. Generous pours, too, if you've got a taste for that. I laughed, said yeah I knew the place a little. It had been about forever since I'd had a drink, and I had to say the idea of getting a little buzz on and rambling in that cherry Ford, windows down, little radio going, appealed to me so much that I didn't let myself question why he'd make such a suggestion. Booze went against everything Ninth Day was about. Alcohol numbs the senses and distances you from the present moment. It makes you nostalgic, which, according to Ninth Day scripture, is the first sign of a slowing movement toward the Vision.

I wonder now what would have happened if I hadn't given in to my dumb thirst, if I'd said no, thanks, and gently closed Barrett's fingers around that twenty, told him I wouldn't want to diminish my connection to the rest of the family. Would they have just changed their plans, like older siblings might when confronted with a day of babysitting the younger ones? Would they have saved everything for some other day, come up with another excuse to get rid of me? Or would they have seen this as a sign that they'd misjudged me? Would I be with them now, somewhere?

But they hadn't misjudged me, of course. My weakness proved that.

Edgar was out by where the truck was parked, tossing feed to the chickens. I nodded at him and then he smiled and said, Say hello to the world for me.

Will do, I was like.

And then he goes, Spread our gospel, Abe.

I opened the door of the Ford and was like, At the library? To which he just shrugged and grinned. I said, All right, man. Got in the truck.

I had two Buds at Sully's and a shot of SoCo and flirted with Martha and actually completely forgot about the library books. Driving back to the farm through the late-summer afternoon, I thought about how lucky I was to have been chosen to be a part of this group, this new family of mine, this tribe.

T.

Tick-tock. All I heard when I came in. The kitchen clock, the one in the shape of an old-fashioned coffee grinder. Then I went into the front room.

I don't know how long I looked at them—seconds, minutes maybe—every one of them naked, in all manner of poses, some splayed out, some on their sides, like they just leaned over for a quick nap. Most of them, I saw once my eyes adjusted to what I was seeing, had vomited on themselves or the floor or both. Millet. Creamed chicken. Candy was on her stomach, her face smashed into the wood floor. Edgar was in this wingback chair in the corner, slumped over, kind of folded into himself. I stepped over a couple people and grabbed him by the shoulders and shook him and said, Edgar! Probably I said, No no no no! He

187

was warm still, but there was no breath, and when I tried to lift him up with my arms under his pits, I couldn't. He sort of fell to the floor and I wiped away the puke from his mouth and started doing CPR as seen on tv. Pressing into his chest and breathing into his mouth. No point, though. I tried with Candy, too, and a couple others, sort of frantic, sort of crying and shaking. After a bit of that I just kind of sat there looking at all their arms and legs flung out or wedged under them. Their faces were barely theirs anymore. Already looked like other things, masks. Empty eyes. Seeing all my dead friends on the floor there I felt a little like when Carlos died when I was twelve. Alone. Like, You fuckers all left me behind?

I got up and must have stood there in the middle of all their bodies for another half a minute, more, before realizing there was no Barrett. Went up the stairs and found him in his room. He was probably listening as I tried to bring the others back from the dead, and I felt kind of embarrassed by that. He was sitting there on his bed, naked like the others, but alive, and with a .38 in his hand. It was almost funny. I saw how small he was—girly shoulders, puny arms, little cock hidden in its poof of fur—and that gun was so chunky that it seemed like he shouldn't even be able to lift it. Finally after about a minute he said, I've really let myself down. And he held the gun out, went, Would you do me a favor? Put a finger to his temple and said, Make it look like it was me, if you can.

Why he didn't just drink the drink like everyone else, I don't know. Probably he watched what happened to them with the puking and all and got scared of going through it himself. Figured a bullet would be quicker. Easier. Kind of a dick move, when you think about it. And then he couldn't even do that.

Send me away and then ask me to finish the job. Okay, motherfucker. Sure. Question my commitment now, why don't you.

U.

Upheaval. What the first doctors called it: psychological upheaval. Why they sent me here instead of the clink. And why the doctors took away my shoelaces and belt and only let me use the plastic forks and knives. Why I'm writing this, I guess.

V.

The Vision. I guess it was God, if you need to think about it that way. I never did. I just thought of it as the point of everything. My mom and dad and the way they are. Carlos getting hit by that train. There was a kid when I was a kid who got some horrible fever that burned out his brain and he came back to school half a mental case, freaking out over the littlest things, screaming until they took him away and his family moved somewhere else and I never saw him again. That kind of thing. Just the goddamn fucking point of it all.

W.

Waste. What everyone says. What a waste.

X.

Xyrem: sodium oxybate, a.k.a. GHB. Everybody at the house (except Barrett) had it in their systems, along with a lot of other stuff.

Also, Xanax. What I'm on right now, along with a lot of other stuff. Moving on.

Y.

Why? What the doctors are always asking me. Not so much why did they do it, but this: if you wanted to go with them, why didn't you turn the gun on yourself? I know what you say, Miss J. You say that I didn't want to die. We sit in our circle and the other guys study their hands and you say that I never did, still don't. You say all I ever wanted was a connection in life, that I never really had that and it's what we all are looking for in all our different ways. And then you sweep your hand around the room and say, Well, what is this?

Z.

Zephyr. What we used to call Edgar's El Camino. The Zephyr. I guess maybe it started because it had this stripe on the side that zigzagged like a Z. I didn't even know what it meant for a long time, but one day I finally looked it up. The west wind. The car was fast and when I think of the happiest times in my life it was cruising outside town with Edgar, down those empty roads. Sometimes we'd have a couple girls hunkered down in the back, trying to keep their hair in place. But mostly not. Mostly it was just us, a little SoCo buzz on, windows open and that wind coming in so I couldn't hear a thing except the ruckus of the engine. Edgar, he's in the driving zone, and neither of us is saying a thing. I felt it, in those times driving with Edgar—even when things were shit at home or I was out of work or it was Carlos's birthday—I felt that this world was so good and wasn't it a trip sometimes, being alive.

And maybe that's what you meant, Miss J., when you said we should look for the grace within the pain. I'm not sure I'm going to find it. I don't know if I have the eyes to see it after everything, or if I even want to, but I guess I'll keep looking a little while longer. For you. Long as I'm here.

ACKNOWLEDGMENTS

. . . .

I want to thank Nicola Mason, Becky Adnot-Haynes, Barbara Neely Bourgoyne, and everyone at Acre Books for their trust and hard work in the creation of this book, as well as my agent Richard Abate for his continuing work and encouragement. Thanks also to the editors and journals who published these stories: Anthony Varallo at *Crazyhorse* ("John Is Alive"); David Daley at *Salon* ("Christmas, West Texas"); Ladette Randolph at *Ploughshares* ("The Caller"); Michael Dumanis at *Bennington Review* ("We've Got Tonight"); and Anna Prushinskaya at *Joyland* ("Glossary for the End of Days").

I would like to acknowledge the support of my friends and colleagues at the University of Louisville, with special gratitude to the rest of the Creative Writing Program, as well as to my students, former and present, whose talent and passion fill me with hope for better days ahead.

A great debt of gratitude is owed to my family, including—but not limited to—Catherine O'Connell, Nick Zivic, Travis Stansel, Robert and Jennifer Strickley, David Lando, and Brooke Lando.

And finally, little would be worth anything without Sarah Anne Strickley, my love and light, and our daughters, Simone and Lila.